"I'm Thinking That Maybe You Believe Sleeping With Me Might Make For Good Publicity.

Or you want the novelty of sleeping with an actress." Had she actually said that? She hadn't even known the fear existed until the words fell out of her mouth.

Sam held up one finger. "First. I don't need you or the damn press in order to be successful. I could buy your family business twice over." He ticked off a second finger. "Second, if I wanted novelty there are other women I could turn to who wouldn't accuse me of chasing them for their money."

Bella's eyebrows shot upward. "You really aren't lacking in ego."

"Women chase me for my money. That's nothing to be proud of."

A hesitant smile tipped her mouth. "I really don't have anything you need."

"Now, there you're wrong." He stepped closer, his body totally flush against hers, his hard muscles a sweet temptation against her.

* * *

Don't miss the exclusive in-book short story by USA TODAY *bestselling author Maureen Child after the last page of* Propositioned Into a Foreign Affair!

Dear Reader,

Thank you for tuning in for the next installment of the Hudson family saga! What a delight it was for me to tell Bella Hudson's story, since she's an actress. Prior to my writing career, I too made my living in the theater—on the stage however, rather than the big screen. After completing my master's degree in theater, I returned to Charleston, South Carolina, and worked at the historic Dock Street Theater.

While my theater days are now long past, I still find my training comes in handy with my books—such as when staging a scene or delving deep into characterization. And best of all, while submerged in the world of creating stories, I get to write the script and direct the show, as well as be all the characters!

Thanks again for picking up Bella's book and happy reading!

Cheers,

Catherine Mann

www.catherinemann.com

CATHERINE MANN

PROPOSITIONED INTO A FOREIGN AFFAIR

Published by Silhouette Books
America's Publisher of Contemporary Romance

Special thanks and acknowledgment to Catherine Mann
for her contribution to
The Hudsons of Beverly Hills miniseries.

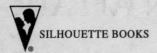

SILHOUETTE BOOKS

ISBN-13: 978-0-373-76940-7
ISBN-10:   0-373-76940-7

Recycling programs
for this product may
not exist in your area.

PROPOSITIONED INTO A FOREIGN AFFAIR

Printed in U.S.A.

Books by Catherine Mann

CATHERINE MANN

RITA® Award winner Catherine Mann resides on a sunny Florida beach with her military flyboy husband and their four children. Although after nine moves in twenty years, she hasn't given away her winter gear! With over a million books in print in fifteen countries, she has also celebrated five RITA® Award finals, three Maggie Award of Excellence finals and a Bookseller's Best Award win. A former theater school director and university teacher, she graduated with a master's degree in theater from UNC-Greensboro and a bachelor's degree in fine arts from the College of Charleston. Catherine enjoys hearing from readers and chatting on her message board—thanks to the wonders of the wireless Internet that allows her to cyber-network with her laptop by the water! To learn more about her work, visit her Web site at www.CatherineMann.com or reach her by snail mail at P.O. Box 6065, Navarre, FL 32566.

To my delightful and talented editor, Diana Ventimiglia.

One

His hands roved her bare body, melting her with the warm heat of his strong caress.

Bella Hudson bit her lip to hold back an embarrassing groan. Barely. She called upon all her training as a Hollywood actress to stay silent while Henri worked his magic on her oiled-up body.

Muscles melting, she buried her forehead deeper in the massage table's face cradle. The scent of aromatherapy candles soothed her nose while Christmas carols sung in French mixed with ocean sounds to caress her ears.

Pure bittersweet pleasure. Very bittersweet.

Sixty-two-year-old masseur, Henri, was likely to be the only man touching her for quite some time since her jerk of an actor boyfriend stomped her heart just last week. And wow, that thought sure kinked up her neck again, encroaching on her peaceful retreat.

She and her precious dog, Muffin, had escaped to France for some much-needed soul soothing at the seaside Garrison Grande Marseille. Garrison hotels always provided the best in pampering, peace and privacy.

And crossing the Atlantic guaranteed she wouldn't risk accidentally running into Ridley or, worse yet, *Uncle David.*

Men. They were all rats. Well, except for Henri, who was too old for her and married, but oh my, he worked wonders with heated river stones along her lower back.

"Henri, are you and your wife happy?" She stared through the face cradle at Henri's gym shoes as he swapped out the stones beside her treasured little Muffin, snoozing away in her pink doggie carrier.

"*Oui*, Mademoiselle Hudson. Monique and I are very 'appy. Four-tee years, three children and ten grandchildren later. My Monique is still beautiful."

He continued to laud his wife and family, his adoration so thick it threatened to smother her.

Or make her gag.

She'd really thought Ridley loved her, only to have him say he'd been too caught up in the romance of their starring roles in the movie about her grandparents' WWII romance. She'd really thought her parents loved each other, too.

Wrong. And wrong again.

Her mother had cheated. She'd slept with her own brother-in-law and now Bella's uncle David was actually her daddy David. Her two cousins were actually her half-siblings. Good God, her family was ripe to be featured on an episode of *Jerry Springer*.

Even river stones couldn't ease that ache.

A low-sounding beep echoed through the room. A series of clicks eched. Had the whale sounds traded up to dolphin calls?

Henri yanked the sheet up to her shoulders. "M'selle Hudson, quick, get up!"

"What?" she asked, not quite tracking yet.

Her eyes snapped open. She blinked to adjust in the dim light and found Henri blocking someone trying to push through the door.

Someone with a camera.

Crap. Crap. Totally tracking now, Bella bolted off the table and to the floor. Her feet tangled in the sheet and she pitched forward.

"Paparazzi. Run!" Henri barked as Bella struggled to regain her footing. "Run. M'sieur Garrison prides himself on protecting the privacy of his clients. He will fire me. Then my wife, she will *keel* me. She is crazy mean when she gets angry."

So much for Henri and Monique's happy marriage.

"Where the hell am I supposed to run to?" Bella spun away from the door—and the camera—making sure to anchor the sheet over her backside. She dashed to Muffin's quilted pink carrier and grasped the handle.

She couldn't wedge past Henri and the photographer struggling to raise his camera over Henri's head.

"The screen," Henri gasped. "Move the screen. There's another door behind. I will hold off this piece of garbage, M'selle Bella."

Henri might have strong hands, but he appeared to be fighting a losing battle. It was only a matter of time before the paparazzi passed him.

Clutching the Egyptian cotton in one hand and the rhinestone-studded carrier in her other, Bella raced to the antique screen painted with Monet-style murals. Sure enough, she found a narrow exit decorated with a large red bow. She butt-bumped the bar, creaked the door open and peeked out.

She looked left and right down an empty corridor, less ornate than the rest of the hotel. Labeled office doors were bedecked with simple holiday wreaths. There might be some after-hours workers around, but running into them beat the hell out of sprinting through the wide-open, high-ceilinged lobby with crystal chandeliers spotlighting her mad dash toward the elevator.

"Okay, Muffin, cross your paws, 'cause here we go."

Her sweet little fur baby yawned.

Bella tucked into the dimly lit hall, empty but for ornately carved antiques. Her bare feet pounded along the thick Persian carpet on her way past a lush green tree, tiny lights winking encouragement. She paused at the first office.

Locked. Damn.

She ran her hand along door after door on her way down. All locked. Double damn.

An echo sounded behind her. The sound of someone running. She glanced over her shoulder and...

Click. Click. Click.

She recognized the sound of a camera in action too well. The short but bulky photographer had over-powered Henri.

Bella ran faster, Muffin's cloth cage bumping against her leg. She wasn't a novice in ditching the press. She'd been aware of the media attention on her family since she was born twenty-five years ago.

Gilded, framed photos of employees stared at her in a weird pseudo voyeurism. She rounded the corner and yes, yes, yes, found a mahogany door slightly ajar. No lights on. Likely empty. She would lock herself inside and call for help.

Panting, she raced the last few steps, slid through the part in the door.

And slammed into a hard male chest.

One without a camera slung over his shoulder, thank heaven, but still a warm-bodied—big-bodied—*man.* She looked up into his cool gray eyes. She didn't need to check the formal photo by the door to confirm the identity of this dark haired, billionaire bachelor. At only thirty-four, he'd already been featured on plenty of "most eligible" lists. This ex-patriate bad boy had broken hearts from the Mediterranean to South Beach.

She'd fallen into the arms of hotel magnate Sam Garrison.

* * *

Sam stared down into the panicked blue eyes of film star Isabella Hudson.

Where the hell were her clothes?

He was used to dealing with eccentric behavior from his star-studded guest list. But a woman running around in nothing more than a sheet? That was a first.

He kept his eyes firmly locked on her panicked face and mussed red hair while waiting for her to clue him in. No need to check out the luscious cleavage on display. He could feel every voluptuous curve of the near-naked beauty pressed enticingly against his chest.

"Media," she gasped, pressing her breasts more firmly against him. "Paparazzi!"

Damn. His libido took a backseat to business. God, he hated the press.

He prided himself on his hotel's privacy, an essential element in attracting high-profile clientele. A breach like this could cost him. Big time. *Nothing* was more important to him than his hotels.

Not even a potentially distracting pair of amazing breasts.

Where was the man she'd been trysting with? Must be a wimp if he'd left her to face the media on her own while clad in nothing more than a sheet, her body slicked up enticingly.

Was the guy married? Or a high-profile politician? His mind raced with possible publicity landmines. This temperamental actress could spell big trouble.

Sam gripped her by the shoulders, her silly, pink dog carrier thumping him in the knee. "Stay in my office. I'll take care of this."

"Thank you. But hurry, please." She backed into the office, her foot peeking out from beneath the sheet to show a gold toe ring. "He's right around the corner—"

Footsteps pounded down the hall.

Sam had spent the past ten years of his life delivering on the promise of privacy and luxury at his branches of the family's exclusive Garrison Grande Resorts. Even a resort magnate had to roll up his sleeves and play bouncer on occasion.

Today, apparently, was one of those occasions.

He stepped back into the empty reception area leading to his office. Waiting. Waiting. Waiting to pounce.

Behind him, he could hear Bella scooping her dog out of the carrier and soothing the restless pet until the bell around the dog's neck quieted.

The footsteps grew louder. Closer.

He stuck an arm out and clotheslined the media hound. Sam lunged out just in time to press a Berluti loafer flat against the guy's chest as he tried to arch up. Bella's dog yipped from inside the office.

Applying more weight, he made sure the burly man became one with the floor. Yeah, he recognized this peon. The guy freelanced for a national gossip magazine.

Or rather he *had* worked. Because by morning, the guy would be fired.

The dog barked louder as if in agreement.

"Security will be escorting you out," Sam growled lowly. "You are no longer welcome here. Your magazine will no longer be given access to any press conferences held here if they keep you on staff."

A big-time loss to the magazine that would guarantee the guy's walking papers.

"I'm just doing my job," the photographer gasped.

"And I am doing mine." Sam pressed his foot down more forcefully.

The guy with the camera cowered. Yeah, he'd gotten the no-trespassing message loud and clear.

Sam eased pressure. "If you manage to land another job, perhaps you will remember to be more *polite* to my guests in the future."

The dog growled, launching through the door and into the hall.

Dog? More like a… Hell, he didn't know what to call the bristly little beast that looked more like a slightly mangy steel wool pad of indeterminable breed.

"Muffin!" Bella squeaked, peeking out the door.

The photographer lurched, grappling for his camera.

Like hell.

Sam yanked the camera from the relentless guy's white-knuckled grip. Muffin leaped with surprising lift for a dog so small. The photographer started to arch upward again. Sam scowled. Muffin landed on the guy's face.

The photographer sagged.

Muffin growled with an underbite and a protruding lower tooth that gave the mutt something close to a Billy Idol snarl. Sam flipped the camera over and popped free the storage disk. He rubbed the tiny bit of plastic between his fingers, his brow furrowed. Then he smiled.

"Muffin," he looked down at the dog, "fetch."

He flicked the card full of six-figure photos to the ugliest little mutt he'd ever seen.

The pooch snapped the "treat" out of midair. *Crunch. Crunch.*

The photographer slumped back with a whimper.

Bella laughed from the doorway. Husky. Uninhibited.

Sam jerked to look over his shoulder at her.

She fisted the sheet tight between her breasts, flame-red hair tumbling down to her shoulders with a post-sex look that called to his libido. No question about it. The American starlet was drop-dead gorgeous. He'd noticed her before when their paths crossed at the occasional high powered party, but her up close appeal now packed an extra punch.

A security guard jogged down the hall, snapping the thread of awareness. "Do you need help, M'sieur Garrison?" Henri the masseur called.

Ah, she'd been getting a massage. He should have guessed, but something about this woman just screamed sex and he'd jumped to conclusions. Regardless, he needed to deal with the crisis at hand.

"Haul this piece of trash out of my hotel and make sure he's never allowed back in." He'd grown up experiencing firsthand what hell these sorts of muckrakers brought to people's lives.

Sam watched the guard drag the dejected photographer into a stairwell, then turned his attention back to the sexy diva.

She knelt beside her dog, sheet cupping the sweet curves of her bottom. "Muffin, give it up." She pinched at the memory card clenched in the pup's snaggletoothed mouth. "I appreciate your help, sweetie pie, but I don't want you to choke."

Sam snapped his fingers.

The dog whipped her furry head around, spitting out the plastic card as she hastened to pay attention.

Bella's eyes went wide with surprise. She gathered up her pet, just managing to keep the white sheet from slithering to her feet.

Desire spiked through him, stronger this time, followed by something else. Determination.

Bella Hudson would not be sashaying out of his life anytime soon tonight.

Two

Bella faced her rescuer. Her very hot rescuer.

Muscular Sam Garrison dominated the corridor outside his office with the same authority he reputedly brought to the boardroom. She tried to distance herself by looking at him with a more analytical eye.

His chestnut-brown hair was trimmed military short, his gray gaze more like piercing steel. He appeared strong enough to take on anyone, anywhere, but even with the sleeves of his crisp, white shirt rolled up, he didn't look the sort to dirty his hands with this type of work often. Everything from his perfect haircut to his high-end loafers shouted privilege.

"Thanks bunches for your help with that reporter."

She fisted her hand on the sheet, securing the scant covering, and thrust her other hand out to shake. "I'm Bella Hudson."

Sure he probably already knew who she was. Most people recognized her on sight, thanks to all the pre-publicity for *Honor.* Posters with her face were plastered all over the U.S., U.K. and France. But it seemed rude to assume someone already knew who she was. Besides, she liked life to be as normal as possible.

Well, as normal as it could be for a girl sprinting around in nothing more than a sheet as she escaped a rabid reporter.

"I know who you are." He extended his hand. "Sam Garrison."

"I know who *you* are," she echoed, her hand sliding into his callused grip, enfolded in heat, hidden from sight by the size of his hold.

Oh, boy.

Any hopes of staying aloof scampered away like leaves in the fall wind. Not that she felt cold. *Nooo.* Heat tingled up her fingers, infusing warmth through her veins from tip to toe. Too much. She'd come here to escape these sorts of feelings, damn it.

Bella snatched her hand back. "Uh, so," she shifted from bare foot to foot, "where did a rich dude like you learn street-fighting moves like that?"

The hotel mogul Garrisons were reputed to be worth more than even her family, who'd made their money from Hudson Studio's box-office hits. From European boarding schools to holidays in Fiji, she hadn't exactly grown up without means, but the Garrisons had wealth that ran deeper with houses around the world. They had a Rolls Royce lifestyle all the way.

"Wealthy people don't know how to fight?" He urged her through his office door into the empty reception area, out of the hallway and away from possible onlookers who might straggle through even after regular work hours.

"That's what bodyguards are for." She just hadn't expected to need one inside a Garrison Grande spa, for crying out loud.

"I fight my own battles—always have." His steely eyes went harder for a flash before he smiled.

Suddenly she felt very, very alone with him since everyone else must have clocked out for the night. That left her alone with Sam Garrison in the lush reception area leading to his office just beyond the open door. Alone with a very sexy male at a time when by all rights she should be swearing off *any* guy, much less this one, a known ladies' man.

She'd met him briefly a few times in the past since the Hudsons and Garrisons frequented many of the same fund-raisers, parties and galas. It was a part of the whole networking game for their high-powered families to be seen in all the right places.

Sure she'd registered he was handsome in the past, but given he was nearly ten years older than her, he'd been out of her range before. What made him so much more compelling tonight? All he'd done was clothesline a reporter.

A shiver of excitement tripped up her spine.

She kept her expression bland—thank goodness for those acting skills of hers. The rogue attraction must be a by-product of raw and vulnerable emotions after her breakup. Not to mention the shock of learning about her uncle and her mother's long-ago affair.

All the more reason to retreat to her room for a bubble bath. Far, far away from any man until she had her equilibrium back. "Thanks again for coming to my rescue. Now how can I get back to my room without flashing the entire lobby?"

"My apologies for this mess." He knelt to scoop up Muffin then crossed to tuck the dog back into the carrier. Had he even heard her question? "We pride ourselves on privacy for our clientele. Rest assured the breach in security will be investigated and addressed."

"It's all right." Stepping on the edge of the sheet, she kicked her foot free and shuffled across to take Muffin's carrier from Sam. "I certainly don't enjoy being hounded by the press, but I understand it's the price I pay for having been born into this family and doing the job I love. Most of the time it's okay." She paused to clear the hitch in her throat. "I'm just having an especially tough month."

He kept his hand on top of the dog carrier, preventing her from picking it up. "Then please give me a chance to make your month take a turn for the better."

Whoa, hold on there, buster. She backed a step from the gleam in his eyes, her heel sinking deep into the lush carpet. "Getting me some clothes to wear would certainly help. I don't even want to risk going out into the hall."

"I have an elevator right through there in my office that will take us straight up to my suite." He stepped closer. "My staff can deliver your clothes there, and dinner, too."

"Dinner?" she squeaked.

He didn't push nearer this time. He simply smiled, his steely, gray eyes glinting with appreciation. "Our chef is internationally known. I will instruct him to make anything you request."

What about a hamburger to go? Because she should run, run, run. Run back to her penthouse for more spinsterish plans—watching a chick flick with Muffin, her third in as many days. Where again she would probably cry her eyes out. Where—yet again—she would see the beautiful French sunrise all by her lonesome.

How flipping pathetic. She needed something to jar her out of that sad routine. She needed to prove she wasn't falling apart.

She eased her grip on the dog carrier and reassessed Sam Garrison. Perhaps he could provide just the distraction she really needed tonight. And it wasn't like there was a chance in hell she would fall for any smooth talker's charms again. Anything that happened between the two of them would be *her* choice with her eyes wide open.

Bella secured her sheet and straightened her shoulders. "Does your cook make doggie treats?"

* * *

He'd lured her to his suite.

With a gourmet meal, a little persuasion and a bit of luck, he would lure her into his bed as well.

Sam sampled the remains of his chardonnay while Bella sat across from him at the intimately small table in the alcove overlooking the moonlit water. Candlelight flickered, casting an ivory glow over her face.

She'd swapped her sheet for a voluminous white robe bearing the hotel's crest on the pocket. Clothes would show up soon—but not too soon. He hadn't seen the need to rush and risk her leaving before he had a chance to persuade her to stay.

The leftovers of their meal remained on the table and antique serving cart. He'd sent away their server after the hotel employee had unveiled the duck in a black currant sauce.

Bella hadn't even blinked. She'd been too busy eating. He liked a woman who enjoyed her food. He'd wondered if the world-class cuisine would be wasted on an anorexic Hollywood type who dined only on watercress and wine.

He had the wine part right.

She alternated sips of his cellar's best with tastes from the wooden board filled with samples of cheeses and fruit. Her face bore the smile of a content woman.

Even her dog was happily snoozing on a pile of gold tasseled pillows on the sofa after snacking on the baked puppy treats his chef had whipped up.

Bella dabbed the corner of her mouth with a linen

napkin. "This was all amazing. Far more relaxing than even a massage." She reached for her wineglass beside the single rose in a vase. The neck of her robe parted slightly to reveal the creamy curves of her breasts. "It's just what I needed after a real bitch of a month."

She had mentioned that in the hall earlier as well. He knew the look of a woman burning to vent and the more she talked, the longer she would stay. Conveniently, that would give him more time to win her over.

He set aside his drink, focusing his total attention on her so she could tell her celebrity tale of woe. An unflattering photo? A former friend spilling lies for a payoff? "Why has your month been so terrible?"

She hesitated for a moment before shrugging. "You must be the only person on the planet who hasn't read a newspaper."

"Gossip magazines you mean?" He spit out the words. "I stay away from them."

"Smart man. I wish my job allowed me that luxury." She downed half the remaining fine wine as if it were nothing more than water. A bracing breath later, she continued, "My grandmother has breast cancer, my boyfriend dumped me and my uncle's really my dad."

He whistled low and long. Not what he'd expected at all. "That *is* one helluva month."

She glanced up from her drink. "Thank you."

"For what?"

"For not offering platitudes that really don't fix anything." She set her crystal stemware back on the table. "I prefer a no B.S. attitude."

He simply nodded, refilling her glass. He hadn't realized the family matriarch—Lillian Hudson—was battling for her life. Lillian was somewhat of a legend around France, her homeland until she met and married a young American soldier during WWII. "This is your grandmother you made the movie about?"

"Yes. Since my grandfather died thirteen years ago, Grandmere—I'm the only one to call her Grandmere, actually, but that's besides the point." Bella paused to sip her wine. "She's made it her mission to bring their wartime love story to the big screen. We were afraid she couldn't live long enough, but with the film making its debut in a week on Christmas day, it looks like she'll have her wish. She's weak, but hanging on. This project has come together in time to celebrate the sixtieth anniversary of Hudson Studios. It's perfect timing."

"It must have been tough playing your grandmother in the movie, especially now." He didn't keep up with Hollywood bios, but he seemed to recall that while Bella Hudson had made great strides in independent films she'd yet to achieve a breakout role.

She toyed with her napkin, twisting it tight. "People think my casting was some kind of family gift, but I had to fight to get that part. And I'm so glad I got the chance. Making a movie about my grandparents' World War II romance was an honor—all the more fitting since the movie itself is called *Honor*. Are you familiar with their story?"

"Only what I've read in news releases about the

movie." He lied a bit, but hearing her sexy voice stoked his senses. And talking about her grandparents softened the strained edges around her eyes.

He suspected the telling would relax her far more than any wine and he most definitely wanted to make Bella feel at home.

She eased back into her chair, toying with the stem on her wineglass. "My grandfather was a U.S. soldier when he met my grandmother here in France. She was a struggling cabaret performer. They secretly married. After the war, he brought her back to the States. My grandfather Charles founded a movie studio so Grand-mere Lillian could bring her talents to the big screen. He made her a legend and she made his fledgling studio a huge success. It's a fairy-tale story." Her eyes sparkled more than the crystal in the candlelight.

"Sounds like you have romance in your genes."

Her smile faded fast. She rose from her chair, taking her drink with her as she turned her back to him and crossed to the window, boats bobbing in the busy French port outside.

"My belief in romance took a serious hit recently." Her voice trembled. "My mother had an affair with her husband's brother. My parents have split up as a result. I always thought they had such a great marriage and now everything has come crumbling down."

He shoved back his chair and walked over to her, stopping an inch shy of touching her. "I'm sorry to hear that."

She glanced over her shoulder at him, fiery spirit

replacing any tears in her eyes. "I'm not sure why I'm spilling my guts to you this way."

"Maybe you just needed to tell someone rather than having the press tell it all for you."

She tossed her head, her hair a flame-red contrast against the white robe. "Perhaps."

The exotic perfume of her shampoo mingled with the scent of the massage oil slicking her skin. His body stirred in response, but he could control himself.

The payoff would be worthwhile for both of them if she decided to stay—and it needed to be her decision. "I'm afraid I don't have any reassuring words to offer you, Bella. My Garrison cousins are all jumping on the marriage bandwagon, but I'm still a cynical soul when it comes to tying the knot."

She laughed low, her eyes lingering on his face a second longer than casual interest. "Did your parents have a crummy marriage, too?"

He slid around to stand beside her, leaning one shoulder on the picture window overlooking the Mediterranean Sea. He normally didn't roll out his life story for strangers, not that his private life was any secret after the way the press raked his mother over the coals. Anything he said, Bella could find out on her own.

So why not use those same facts to wrangle his way a little closer to her? It wasn't like any of the information upset him anymore.

He stuffed his hands in his pockets to keep from reaching for her too soon and risk spooking her. "My parents never had a marriage at all. My father was a scam artist looking to hook up with a wealthy Garrison. Mom fell for him at first, got pregnant, but wised up before actually tying her life to the jerk."

Her hand fluttered to rest on his arm. "I'm sorry, for your mother and for you."

"No loss on my part. He's an ass. He tried to get custody of me once, but everyone knew he was only interested in the trust fund that came with me. The courts threw out his case once three women showed up with marriage licenses bearing my dad's name."

"He'd been married before?"

"But never divorced."

"Ouch," she gasped. "Your father was a bigamist?"

"*Big* time." This wasn't something he talked about, but if sharing it would gain him traction in winning over Bella, then why not? He'd long ago hardened himself to the facts that made up his parent-age. "Mom was forty-one, single, pregnant and hounded by the press."

Her eyes went wide. "Your mother was forty-one when she had you? From the way you told the story I thought she was younger."

His mother had once told him that she hated being a cliché most of all—the old maid taken in by a younger Lothario. Sam hated most of all that the press had hammered home that image to his mother. They'd made her life miserable to the point she'd become a recluse, living in a barrier island bungalow off the coast of Southern Florida.

He stared back at young and vibrant but too vulnerable Bella. Would the media wear her down? Or would she develop Teflon defenses over time?

And speaking of relationships and breakups…
"You mentioned an ex-boyfriend."

She looked down and away, out the window again. "My costar in *Honor.* Ridley the Rat."

He stroked a strand of her hair back over her shoulder, leaving his hand there, caressing the inside curve of her neck. "Ridley the Rat, huh? I'm glad he's out of the picture."

Bella studied him through narrowed eyes, but she didn't pull away. "Your empathy factor is sadly lacking."

He slid his fingers into her hair, cupping her head. "But my attraction factor is not. Ridley the Rat is an idiot."

"Oh." Her pupils widened and she swayed closer toward him in unmistakable attraction.

Enough dancing around the subject. Time to let her know how much she affected him and see if she felt the same. He dipped his head and skimmed his mouth over hers. Her breathy sigh, and the downward glide of her eyelashes encouraged him.

He traced the seam of her lips until she parted for him and finally her hands slipped up his arms to rest on his shoulders. A jolt of desire shot through him, instantaneous. Undeniable. He deepened the kiss, stroked, searched, learned the taste and feel of her.

She edged closer to him, returning his kiss with

an enthusiasm that made him hard with desire. Her soft curves grazed his chest, her fluffy robe warm from her heat. He could keep pushing the point and he was fairly certain she would follow him all the way into his bedroom a simple door away. Her response indicated as much. But he needed to *hear* her total, unreserved surrender.

Sam eased his mouth from hers, his hands sliding down her back to loop loosely around her waist. He watched her, waiting for her to open her eyes again.

Finally, her lashes fluttered open again, her blue gaze passion glazed. "Wow."

Yeah, "wow" pretty much summed it up. He wasn't sure what it was about her kiss that sent him so high so fast, but this woman packed a hell of a punch to his libido. He didn't want to think overlong how much a simple kiss rocked him. He gathered up his shaky control and focused on winning her over for what he wanted most.

More.

More of her.

Tonight.

"Wow," she said again, her voice steadier this time.

He glided his knuckles along her jaw, the silky feel of her skin making him ache all the way to his teeth. He wanted to discover if she felt this good all over. "My eyes followed you more than once at parties we both attended over the years. But you don't need me to tell you what a gorgeous woman you are when there are magazine covers devoted to stroking your ego."

"I hardly know you." Yet her face dipped toward
his touch. "You're polite and this dinner was lovely,
but I'm not even sure I like you."

"Ah, but do you *want* me?"

Three

Bella gripped the edge of the winter-cool windowsill to keep from falling straight into Sam's muscular arms. Even the romantic Marseille skyline twinkling beyond the pane seemed to be special-ordered for seduction. With the power of his kiss still zinging through her veins, she couldn't deny the obvious to him, much less to herself.

She wasn't sure why he affected her so much, so quickly. She didn't like to think of herself as shallow, falling into bed with a man because of his looks. But then hadn't she done just that with Ridley?

God, even thinking of how easily he'd tossed her aside still hurt. Ridley had said he loved her. He'd even discussed getting married. All lies, lies she hadn't seen through because she'd been too caught in the romantic air of filming her grandparents' story. She'd been ripe for the picking when Ridley showered her with his flowery charm.

Apparently he was an even better actor than she'd given him credit for.

She scrubbed memories of him from her brain. Thoughts of him now, while she was with Sam, felt disloyal somehow. For tonight, in this moment, she would be totally with this man, a man who issued bold, blunt statements of fact rather than fake, empty, flattery.

Yes, she wanted Sam. Yes, she needed something to ease the pain inside her and it seemed being with him might help her forget for at least a night. But no way could she let him think she was a total pushover.

She tipped her chin, the heat of his touch still tingling. "You're certainly not lacking in the ego department."

He trailed a finger along the lapel of her bathrobe. "I'm only stating facts here. You're a gorgeous woman. I would have to be dead not to notice."

His words soothed her wounded ego. People complimented her often enough, but so many of them were sycophants and suck-ups, she discounted much of what they said. She couldn't miss the straightforward sincerity in Sam's eyes.

Still, a wounded part of her needed to push. "A person's worth is about more than looks."

"Of course." He stepped closer, the tangy scent of

his aftershave tempting her to breathe deeper. "But initial, animal attraction shouldn't be discounted."

"Is that what's happening here?" she asked, even when she already knew the answer to that one.

She was completely out of her depth, wavering on weak-kneed hunger for him, and it was a feeling unlike any she'd ever experienced. Animal attraction sounded just about right for her instinctual need to touch him.

"What do you think?" He rested his hands lightly on her shoulders, broad palms gently massaging away her tension.

And self-control.

"I'm thinking that maybe you believe sleeping with me might make for good publicity, or that you want the novelty of sleeping with an actress." Had she actually said that? She hadn't even known the fear existed until the words fell out of her mouth.

"Damn, lady, that's a hefty load of insecurities." He gave her shoulders a final squeeze before pulling his hands back. "Let's unpack that one issue at a time." He held up one finger. "First, I don't need you or the damn press in order to be successful. I'm managing quite fine on my own. In fact, I could buy your family business twice over." He ticked off a second finger. "Second, if I wanted novelty, there are other women I could turn to who wouldn't accuse me of chasing them for their money."

Her eyebrows shot upward. "You really aren't lacking in ego."

"Women chase me for my money. That's nothing to be proud of."

A hesitant smile tipped her mouth. "I really don't have anything you need."

"Now, there you're wrong." He stepped closer, his body totally flush against hers, his hard muscles a sweet temptation against her.

"I am?" she gasped, the musky scent of him swirling through her with that one breath.

"Since the second I saw you running down that hall, I have wanted to get closer to you. So much so that I'm damn near about to explode if I don't get my mouth on some part of you soon."

The intensity of his rumbling voice stroked her senses as artfully as his touch, his kiss, everything about this moment drugging her, dragging her away from any good intentions.

She knew he had a reputation with women, and in a strange way that made this encounter somehow safe. She didn't have to worry about risking a relationship. Her heart wouldn't be in jeopardy.

Casual affairs had never been her style, but then her life had never been this upside down. Why not take what she needed? What he so clearly wanted, too.

Maybe she'd been hoping for a little adventure when she'd taken the elevator up to his private suite tonight. But then, perhaps being wrapped in Sam Garrison's arms was the balm her wounded spirit needed. And who better to seek this moment of mindless pleasure with than a man who knew all about the joys of hot, one-time encounters?

"Birth control?" she asked, that issue the last hurdle between her and jumping into his bed.

"In the other room." His hand slid behind her back, anchoring her against him. "Is that a yes?"

She touched his face, her fingers testing his raspy five-o'clock shadow. "Yes, definitely yes."

A low growl of appreciation his only response, he scooped her off her feet and carried her across the sitting area to the door ajar, leading into his bedroom. Dim lighting from the crystal chandelier showcased the king-size bed with a large painted panel of the French countryside over the bed.

The burgundy-and-gold brocade comforter was turned back invitingly. Champagne waited in a bucket by the bed along with chocolate-covered strawberries.

She thumped him on the shoulder lightly. "You were planning this all along when you placed the order for supper?"

"What can I say? I was hopeful as hell from the second you slammed into my chest wearing nothing more than a sheet."

So he'd been hopeful. Yet he'd still given her plenty of chances to say no. He might be a player, but he was a player with honor.

Time to stop thinking.

Time to feel and forget.

Raising her face for his kiss, she smoothed her hands over his hair, finally allowing herself the indulgence of feeling its texture. Soft along the top, a bit bristly as his hair tapered off at his neck. She savored the pleasure of being kissed by a man who knew how to do it so beautifully well.

Beside the sprawling king-size bed, he lowered her to her feet, her toes nearly disappearing in the carpet. Her hands roved his back, the fine fabric of his shirt soft against her fingers, a thin barrier over the hard muscled expanse. A thin barrier she quickly unbuttoned and stroked away to reveal the cut of muscles, more defined than she'd imagined. And her imagination had been darn impressed.

What other pleasant surprises waited for her? He had far more clothes on than she did and she did not intend to be the only one naked in this room.

Desperation gripped her with a frantic need to soak up everything she could from her time with him. This was her amnesia drug of choice. A way to forget everything. A way to relieve the tension Henri had said riddled her muscles. She couldn't imagine herself in a relationship anytime soon and she couldn't see herself indulging in a string of meaning-less encounters. This, *Sam,* could be her last chance for the sweet pleasure of a man's bold stroke for quite a while to come.

He kissed his way down the sensitive curve of her neck, nudging aside her robe with his chin, only an inch. She'd expected him to whip away the belt quickly. Instead he took his time, lavishing attention in the curve of her shoulder.

"Faster," she said, unbuckling his pants frantically as he toed off his shoes and socks.

"Slower," he commanded, lowering her to the bed, sinking her into the downy fullness. Her robe parted. He froze for an instant before he exhaled hard. "I knew you were beautiful, and it's obvious you have a great body, but damn. Just damn."

Maybe he was only dishing out flattery to win her over… Hey wait, he didn't have to win her over anymore. She was already naked and ready in his bed.

Unwilling to wait any longer, she arched up and hooked her thumbs in his waistband. "How about we get rid of those pants so I can enjoy you, too?"

His hands covered hers as she swept away his trousers and boxers, the bristly hair on his muscular thighs sending a shower of awareness stinging through her. She let her eyes rove him in a "wow" moment all her own. His broad shoulders spoke of strength beyond the boardroom, a strength she'd experienced firsthand when he'd so effortlessly carried her. She glanced back up to his angular face— handsome in a stark way—softened by an intriguing dimple in his chin.

In a flash of insight, she realized she'd chosen Ridley's opposite. Other than dark hair, Sam shared little in common with her more wiry, smoothly good-looking ex-lover. She shoved away thoughts of another man.

No one and nothing else would intrude on this.

Sam tapped her on the shoulder lightly, encouraging her to fall back on the mattress. He snagged a bottle of champagne from an ice bucket beside the bed. Deftly, he popped the magnum, angling it over her body so the frothy overflow splashed along her stomach.

"Sam!" she squealed at the cold kiss of bubbles against her overheated flesh.

He dribbled champagne along her stomach. Cool droplets gleamed on her skin, sending a shiver through her. He dipped his head to taste and tease her with his tongue. Lower, lower and lower still he slowly dribbled a thin trail of amber liquid between her legs.

Wicked determination lit his eyes as he tasted her. Carefully, again and again, just enough to tease her higher without sending her over the edge.

He glanced up at her with heavy lidded eyes. "You make me drunk."

"We didn't have *that* much wine with dinner." She wouldn't be able to delude herself later that this had been an alcohol-induced mistake.

He gripped her hips, his naked body sliding up and over hers. "You misunderstand. I said '*you* make me drunk.'"

"*You* flatter me."

"I am known for being brutally honest."

His undisguised admiration numbed her bruised ego more effectively than any bottle of champagne. Bella flipped Sam to his back, leaned toward the silver tray by the ice bucket and plucked up a chocolate-covered strawberry between her teeth. She brought her mouth to his and shared.

He nipped at the fruit, closer and closer until their lips met. His kiss tasted of strawberries and champagne, and she couldn't deny the power of his touch along her skin. His touch brought the perfect forgetfulness.

Sam held her kiss while reaching to the bedside table for protection. He sheathed himself before she even had time to totally register what he was doing, but grateful all the same that he'd possessed a whisper of restraint enough to do so.

He gripped her hips and positioned her over him, nudging against her as he stared up into her eyes. Slowly, she lowered herself onto him, taking him, letting him take her with bold strokes that scattered any remaining rational thought.

Heat rose and she threw herself into that swirl of sensation. Total oblivion. Complete forgetfulness of all the things that had driven her here in the first place. Into his bed.

She writhed more urgently against him, ready for release, almost there already…. He flipped her to her back and took control and kept that sweet finale from her, coaxing her to the edge again and again until her fingernails scored his back.

Still, he tormented her by slowing the pace, damn him. She'd had enough of men ruling her life and her emotions. She would take what she wanted, *when* she wanted it.

Bella locked her legs around his hips, sensation rolling through her as fast as their wet bodies slid against each other. Almost… Almost…

There.

Her muscles tensed as pleasure pulsed through her so hard and fast a cry burst free. Dimly she registered his hoarse growl of completion as she rode the wave into total satisfaction.

Replete, she sagged beneath him into the fluffy comforter. The scent of champagne, strawberries and lovemaking filled the air, but she knew it would all fade soon enough.

Her escape from reality would end at sunrise.

Sun peeking on the horizon, Sam tucked the sheet more securely around Bella as he carefully slid from the bed. Her hair splayed over the pillow, her bare arm gripping the coverlet as if securing it for another great escape.

Muffin stared at him quietly from the foot of the bed, wide eyes unblinking, Billy Idol snarl in place. He'd never been much of a dog person, but at least the mutt wasn't an annoying yippy barker.

He shifted his attention back to Bella. No question that Ridley guy had done a number on her ego. The rat's timing sure sucked, with her grandmother's illness and her true parentage coming out.

She'd mentioned the press had already started printing stories about the mess. Media hounds would eat up her misfortune faster than wolves devoured a fresh carcass. The very reason he preferred to stay as far away from them as possible.

By all rights he should say goodbye to Bella once she woke. He'd certainly intended to when planning out this seduction.

He'd expected great sex. But he hadn't expected to want more.

She'd made it clear this was a one-night-only deal for her, too. Now he had to convince her otherwise.

He wasn't sure how long it would take for them to work each other out of their system. He wasn't even sure how long he could put up with the media circus that would undoubtedly follow her wherever they went together.

The one thing he did know? He would have to tread warily with her, given her recent experience with men. Of course, he wasn't an inept jackass like that Ridley moron.

A soft knock sounded from beyond the sitting area, out in the hall.

Right on time.

Sam shrugged into his robe and strode past the remains of their meal to answer the door. Bella's mutt pattered across the floor to join him. Sam blocked the pup with his foot.

His personal assistant, a middle-aged Englishman, stood in the hall, his eyes going wide for a flash at the sight of the dog. "Here are the clothes you ordered for Miss Hudson, along with a new room key."

"Thank you, Parrington." Sam stayed in the entry,

not wanting to expose Bella to the other man's eyes. "And the security breach?"

"One of the ladies at the registration desk started dating the photographer a couple of weeks ago." Parrington reached for the PDA clipped to his belt. "I have the name here."

"No need to tell me now. Just send the information to my e-mail. The guy probably seduced the woman for her connections here." A self-serving ass just like his own father. "Thank you for looking into this. I appreciate that no more stress will be visited on Bella Hudson while she is with us."

"Rest assured." His assistant nodded crisply.

"Good. Good. Well done." Sam closed the door again and stared back into the bedroom at Bella. She still slept soundly.

His body stirred at just the sight of her. He wasn't sure what made her different, but he still wanted her even after their night filled with lovemaking and what he wanted, he got.

He knew she'd only slept with him as a balm to her bruised ego. No doubt she planned to hotfoot her way out of here when she woke. Most times, that would have been a relief. But he wasn't ready to say goodbye to her yet. He had other plans.

Plans to delay her leaving France.

Plans to get her back in his bed.

Mind set, he picked up the phone and dialed.

* * *

Bella picked through the layers of sleepy fog until she could pry her eyes open. She blinked twice and...

Oh, my God. She'd really slept with Sam Garrison because sure enough, she could hear him in the shower. What the hell had she been thinking?

She scrubbed her tousled hair off her forehead and stretched, her body tender from a night of uninhibited lovemaking. She eyed the empty champagne bottle and a fast flush heated her face. She eyed the clock and groaned again at how late she'd slept.

What seemed like such a good idea last night now seemed totally reckless. How could she have thought she could sleep with a man without giving something of herself?

The shower turned off.

No, no, no, she wasn't ready to face him yet, wasn't sure if she would ever be. All of her reasons for jumping into bed with him—her breakup, her parents' marital train wreck—now had her eying the door for a fast escape before she risked even a corner of her already bruised heart.

She inched quietly out of the bed, farther and farther until one leg slipped off the mattress. She toed the floor and eased herself the rest of the way out from under the covers. Careful not to make a sound. Determined to get away before he finished his shave and she had to make morning-after talk with a man she barely knew but had slept with anyway.

She prided herself on being so much better than many of the promiscuous Hollywood party types.

Hell, she'd even managed to keep her clothes on in her movies so far. She was a *serious* actress, a deep person who rescued pound puppies rather than spending a gazillion dollars on a vanity pet.

And yet at the first sign of heartache, she'd thrown away her clothes and inhibitions.

Speaking of clothes, she needed something to wear. She would settle for the robe, if need be—

Her gaze fell on a stack of clothes resting on the gold-striped sofa, Muffin resting her head on top of the pile. Bella raced across the room for the jeans and frilly top—hers. Sam must have sent someone into her room.

She scruffed Muffin's head before gently moving the dog aside. "Sh… Stay quiet, sweetie."

Under the dog's head, a room card rested on top of the clothes. Thank goodness. With a little luck and a lot of stealth, she could make it out of here undetected with her pet.

She scooped up the clothes. Sam's thoughtfulness tugged at her.

Or was Sam just eager to see her leave by making sure her clothes were ready? Insecurity nipped her heels harder than Muffin bounding after her, bell around her neck chiming.

"Shhh, shhh, shhh, Muffin."

Bella took off the collar so the bell wouldn't chime and alert him to her escape. She would put it on again once she returned to her room.

No way in hell did she plan to be featured in any

photos—or relationship—with one of the world's most eligible bachelors.

She slipped on the clothes and her gold Escada sandals quickly, tucked Muffin back in her carrier and made a beeline for the door. Half in, half out, she stared back at the bathroom door. Wistfulness whispered through her. What if they'd showered together?

God, she was a sucker. "What if" nothing. They'd enjoyed amazing sex, two adults who wanted no ties.

It was over.

She closed the door behind her and took the elevator to the penthouse floor. Almost home free. She should walk Muffin, but she wasn't ready to be seen in public yet. She turned to the elevator operator….

He nodded. "Do you need help with your little pet, mademoiselle?"

She loved it when people read her mind. "Yes, thank you. She just needs a quick walk. Her leash is looped on the side of her cage here," she rattled off instructions at light speed as if that would bring about her escape all the faster. She passed over Muffin's carrier, blowing a kiss to her little sweetie.

The elevator dinged, the doors opened and she raced the last few feet to her door, ready for a shower, fresh clothes—and a new hotel. She whipped her key card in and out, shoved open the door.

And she came face-to-face with the last person she expected to see.

Four

Bella gripped the door to her hotel suite, resisting the urge to bolt back into the hall. It wasn't like she had to face a pack of wolves. Seated on the floral loveseat was her cousin Charlotte, thumbing through a newspaper, one of her favored Jamin Puech beaded purses beside her.

A cousin who was actually her half sister since they shared the same father.

What a convoluted family tree. Bella had three brothers she'd grown up with, and now her two cousins were actually half siblings.

Charlotte Hudson Montcalm lived with her French aristocrat husband at the Chateau Montcalm, a palatial estate outside Provence, a fair ways from this port city. What in the world was she doing in Marseille?

And more particularly why was she in Bella's hotel suite, sitting there as serenely perfect as the white calla lilies on the coffee table in front of her?

She loved Charlotte, but wasn't ready to deal with their changed relationship. Sorting through the tumultuous emotions would take time. She wasn't ready to see *anyone* associated with her tangled family tree.

Then why had she decided to hide out in the very country where her cousin/half sister lived with her husband Alec?

Bella sighed, wishing that annoying voice of reason niggling at the back of her mind would take a nap. Freudian slips were a real pain in the butt.

She closed the door behind her and stepped deeper into the sitting area. Light streamed through the window, whispery gold curtains pulled wide to reveal the harbor with sailboats and ringed with quaint whitewashed buildings.

Pulling a smile, Bella opened her arms for a hug, determined to act as normal as possible. "Hello, Charlotte. What a pleasant surprise to find you here waiting for me."

Her cousin's signature perfume reminded her of summer vacations together, staying up late and trying out makeup together.

"And hello to you, too." Charlotte stood, her stomach large with her advanced pregnancy. Still the blond-haired, blue-eyed beauty carried herself with her usual sophistication. They were the same age and during their teenage years, Bella had felt freckled and chubby next to her willowy cousin.

Bella hugged her taller cousin—sister. Damn, it was tough to rewire a lifetime of programming.

Easing back, she reminded herself none of this was Charlotte's fault. "What are you doing here so far from home?"

Bracing a hand behind her on the arm of the sofa, Charlotte lowered herself back to sit again. "Alec and I flew over this morning to shop for the baby and learned you were here, too."

An odd coincidence, but Charlotte's serene smile showed no sign of subterfuge. Alec had planes at his disposal ready to be used at a moment's notice.

Charlotte pulled back, her brow puckered with worry. "Why didn't you tell me you were in Marseille?"

Bella sat in the tapestry wingback chair. A light breakfast had already been laid out on the antique tea cart—small baguettes, jams and fresh fruit beside a carafe of coffee, starched linen napkin lying beside the silver tray.

The thought of food churned her already nervous stomach. "Would you like something to eat?"

"Does a bird sing? Of course I would like something to eat." She grinned. "I'm pregnant."

Bella watched as Charlotte tore off a piece of bread. "How did you find out I'm staying at the Garrison Grande?"

Charlotte smoothed her hands over her baby belly. "Alec heard it from one of his business contacts."

The truth exploded in her mind. "From Sam Garrison."

Charlotte's silence and neutral smile answered clearly. She swirled the silver knife through the glistening preserves and smoothed a dollop of raspberry jam on top of her bread.

But when would Sam have had time to do this? They'd only met up the night before and they'd spent every waking moment together....

Charlotte speared a melon ball. "Okay, yes, he called early this morning."

While she'd been sleeping, before his shower. The only question was had Charlotte truly already been here shopping or had she dropped everything to fly over just because Sam sent up an SOS. Regardless, her half sister had gone to a lot of trouble for her. Bella poured a cup of black coffee and took a sip to wash down the lump in her throat.

"I appreciate your stopping by, but why would Sam call you?"

She barely knew the man and already he was tampering with her life. She'd come here to feel closer to her grandmother. If she'd wanted to see her sister, she would have called her. Now she was stuck in an awkward situation where she appeared rude.

Charlotte waved the silver jelly knife lightly. "Who knows what men think most of the time? I do know that you shouldn't be staying at a hotel. You should be at the estate with Alec and me."

Damn, damn, damn Sam for interfering. "I didn't want to risk bringing the media down on you. Stress is the last thing a pregnant woman needs."

"I'm completely healthy—and ravenous." She popped the last pinch of bread into her mouth. She chewed slowly before saying, "Are you staying away from me because of our father?"

Bella snapped back in her seat. She hadn't expected ever-poised Charlotte to be so blunt. Hearing the truth of her parentage still cut straight through to her heart.

"Why would I do that? Mother and Uncle—" she winced "—David are the ones at fault, not you. They're the ones who cheated on their spouses."

"Looking at me could make you remember we're half sisters rather than cousins." Her blue eyes darkened with pain.

For the first time, Bella considered how all of this must have hurt Charlotte. David Hudson hadn't been much of a father, always too busy to spend any time with Charlotte or her brother, but he was still their father. The way he'd torn apart the fabric of their family with his betrayal was terrible.

Bella mentally kicked herself for being so self-centered in her grief. Charlotte deserved reassurance. She reached past the wooden tea cart to squeeze her hand.

"I loved you before; I love you now." As she said the words, she realized they were true.

Her issue was with their father, David. How strange to think she wouldn't be here without him, yet at the same time it felt as if he'd stolen her real father from her—Markus, the man who'd brought her up, the man who'd declared her Daddy's pampered girl, the man who'd been kept in the dark for years just as she had.

Until the whole ugly secret had come to light.

Blinking back tears, she snatched the rolled linen napkin from the silver tray and dabbed her eyes. She was tired of crying over this. She needed to quit feeling sorry for herself and move on. "I'm sorry. You're right that I was avoiding you. I have to confess, I wasn't sure if I could even speak to anyone about this without crying."

Yet somehow she'd managed to tell Sam the whole sad and sordid tale. Memories of strawberries and champagne bubbled in her brain, stirring a phantom taste on her tongue.

Charlotte clasped Bella's hand. "It's just going to take a while to settle into this new family tree."

Was it wrong to want the old one back? Was it wrong to be damned indignant on Markus's behalf? So much anger could sour her insides quickly. She could sure use some of Charlotte's serenity right about now.

"Wise words." Bella nodded, ready to talk about anything but this. "How do you feel? Is everything going well with the pregnancy?"

"Totally perfect. I'm huge, but happy." Her joy sparkled as brightly as her diamond ring catching the sun when she straightened her pearls. "Alec is spoiling me shamelessly. He even says pregnancy is sexy." She rolled her eyes. "I laugh, but I'm secretly soaking it up. It's no secret I had a hard time trusting him after the way our father treated my mother."

Bella tried not to flinch every time Charlotte used the word *father*. How could she ever grow accustomed to thinking of him that way? She'd always thought she had her mother's blue eyes. Now looking into Charlotte's flashing blue gaze, she saw the real source of her eye color.

David Hudson.

She struggled not to cry and risk another outpouring of sympathy from Charlotte that would only make the urge to feel sorry for herself all the stronger. Blast Sam for pressing this on her before she was ready. "Thank you for coming to check on me. That was truly a sweet thing to do. No matter what, we're family."

"I'm glad to hear you say that." Tears filled Charlotte's eyes this time. "I was afraid things would be uncomfortable between us."

"We'll be fine." She wished she could be so certain about how things would work out with the rest of her relatives.

"So will you stay with Alec and me?"

And watch her sister wallow in all that newlywed love and happiness as the two of them waited for their first child?

Not a chance.

Charlotte may have found peace and happiness in

spite of their family's crummy track record with marriage. But Bella just wasn't feeling it for herself.

She patted Charlotte's hand. "Thank you for the generous offer, but I'm afraid I've already hidden out from the press as long as I can. I need to get back to the States for the premiere of *Honor.*"

Charlotte pressed a palm to her back. "Only a few more days until the Christmas debut. I wish I could be there, but a flight that long really wouldn't be wise for me this late."

"Everyone understands. You have to put the baby's health first."

Charlotte's smile wavered. "I just hope our grandmother can hold on long enough to see this baby."

Facing Lillian's impending death was difficult for the whole Hudson clan. Bella felt as if her whole family was falling apart.

Charlotte sniffed. "Enough tears. I'm meeting Alec in an hour. Please, keep in touch."

"Of course, I will." Bella hugged her cousin-turned-sister a final time before walking with her to the door with a farewell wave.

She stayed in the open doorway, watching Charlotte step into the elevator—

Just as Sam stepped out.

Bella gasped and started to back into her room but, oh, my God, she was too late. And hey, wait, she had a bone to pick with him anyway over the heavy-handed way he'd interfered in her life. She stiffened her resolve and waited to face him, toe-to-toe. She had a lot of mixed emotions roiling around inside her these days and he would make a perfect target for a good, old-fashioned shout down to release the pressure.

Sam closed the last few feet between them and walked her backward toward the suite again.

Stopping in the open doorway, she put her hands on her hips and wished she had on heels for height. "Why are you here?"

"Well, good morning to you, too, Bella." He held up his hands, a filmy gold scarf dangling from one, large-framed sunglasses from the other. "I'm here to kidnap you."

From the look on Bella's face, this wasn't going to be as easy as he'd planned.

"Come on," Sam urged, "at least talk to me inside, so we don't risk some reporter seeing us."

Not a chance in hell would that happen here, but she didn't need to know that.

Huffing, she spun on her heel and headed back into her suite. He closed the door behind them.

He'd hoped a visit with her cousin/sister would soften her up, help her deal with some of her frustration. He'd also hoped reminding her of her family connection to this area would entice her to stick around awhile longer. His instincts were never wrong when reading people in the business world. Why should handling Bella be any different?

He would be analytical about this. Emotions were messy and led to mistakes, a truth he'd learned from his failed engagement to Tiffany Jones. He'd certainly missed the boat on reading that woman. She was the daughter of a respected business acquaintance, and Sam had considered settling down after attending yet another wedding for one of his Garrison cousins.

A momentary weakness.

Tiffany wasn't worth his trust. She'd slept with a yachting friend of his, then had the gall to try and blame it on Sam for not paying enough attention to her. He might not be the most attentive man on the planet, but he'd been straight-up honest with her from the start about the demands of his career. She'd responded by accusing him of loving his job more than her.

He'd realized she was right and called it quits between them.

Sam shoved aside doubts. He'd taken care of the Tiffany situation before it spiraled out of control into a lifetime mistake. Thank God they hadn't gotten around to setting a date or sending out invitations. He hadn't totally screwed things up.

And Bella wasn't looking for forever. In fact, he was going to have to work his ass off to wrangle a few weeks with her. She was as committed to her career as he was. That boded well for them.

Although her scowling silence wasn't exactly promising.

Sam looped the gold scarf around Bella's neck playfully. "Come on." He tugged lightly, drawing her deeper into her suite. "Smile."

"Like hell." She whipped the scarf out of his hand and off her neck. "I'm mad at you."

The best defense was a good offense. "If anyone has cause to be angry, it's me. You ran out without saying goodbye. If I'd done that to you, I would be scum. Why is it any different when you skulk off?"

She pitched the wadded scarf at his chest. "You've got to be kidding."

"What?" He snagged the whispery fabric before it slid to the floor. "Only women get to be indignant over someone running out after sex?"

She opened her mouth, then hesitated. Her brow furrowed with confusion. Ah, he had her off-balance. Good. Let her wonder if maybe he wanted some postcoital cuddling.

Bella shoved her tangled hair back from her face. "I'm sorry for not saying goodbye." Her frown shifted into a scowl. "Now you can apologize to me."

"For what?"

She crossed her arms over her luscious chest. "You know what you did."

"I saved you from the press yesterday. Damn, I'm a real bastard."

She jabbed him in the chest with one finger. "You called Charlotte."

"Says who?" he hedged.

"Are you denying it?"

Apparently she knew already, so he confessed, "I'm not denying anything."

He walked past her, deeper into her room, making it tougher for her to usher him out. He ran a cool hotelier's eye over the polished sheen of the antiques, the designs unapologetically European. There might be a forty-six-inch flat screen with surround sound at any given U.S. Garrison Grande, but the curtains here were raw silk and the floors polished bamboo.

Here, he'd cultivated a rich, old-world feel all the way down to the paneled murals on the walls. "I called Alec this morning. I was worried about you."

Her plump lips went tight. "You have to realize from what I told you that my cousin is really my half sister." She dropped into a tapestry wingback chair. "I'll deal with that when I'm good and ready."

He looked around but saw no sign of the padded pink dog crate. "Where's Muffin?"

"One of your helpful staff is walking her."

"Good." He nodded.

"Maybe you can go find her for me," she said, her hint to leave none too subtle.

"About Charlotte…I thought you might need someone to talk to." He plucked a couple of grapes from the breakfast tray and popped them into his mouth.

"That's my decision to make."

"Hey—" he thumped his chest "—I'm trying to be nice here."

"No hidden agendas?"

"Who me?" He pinched up another purple grape.

"Said the spider to the fly."

"Forgive me?" He brought the plump fruit to her

mouth, caressing it along her lips, reminiscent of how they'd fed each other strawberries and champagne.

She bit the grape, nipping his fingers none too gently in the process. "Not yet."

Yet? That meant he had a chance to get in her good graces again, a prospect that became all the more important as even her playful bite sent a bolt of heat straight to his groin.

Bella swallowed the grape, her tongue flicking over her lips.

"What did you mean about kidnapping me?" she asked, her voice throaty and confidential.

Victory shot a second jolt through him almost as strong as desire. "I thought you might like to spend time in France somewhere other than cooped up in a hotel."

Her nose scrunched. "And run through the gauntlet of reporters? I don't think so."

He looped the scarf over her head and dropped the sunglasses in her lap. "Put those acting skills of yours to work and change up your walk a bit, take on an accent. Leave the rest to me. I'm willing to bet you could plow through your entire Christmas shopping list before a single photo is snapped...unless you would rather go home."

She winced.

Good. Score one for his master plan.

"Come on, Bella. I have Christmas shopping of my own to take care of and I could really use your help in choosing something for my mother. So?" he pressed. "Are you in?"

"Well, I haven't had time to shop for gifts." Finally, her face cleared and she sighed. "All right. Find my dog and you can take me shopping."

He held back his smile of victory.

"I need to shower first."

His body stirred at even the thought of her naked under the spray of water. Too bad he couldn't convince her to skip shopping altogether and spend the day in bed together.

She jabbed a finger into his chest. "You are not invited to join me."

"Muffin and I will be waiting."

Five

If only every day could end with coffee and a handsome man, the Eiffel Tower silhouetted in the distance.

Bella tightened the gold scarf draped over her head, but she'd ditched the large sunglasses since the sun was setting. Besides, they were indoors, tucked away in a corner of a small Parisian café. The scent of espresso wound through the restaurant, the soft chatter of native speakers soothed her with its melodious cadences.

So far Sam had done a brilliant job at evading the press, arranging a limo and extra security at one side entrance while spiriting her away to a private car out another. The plan had gone off without a hitch, but then he was full of surprises today.

Sam had told her he intended to take her shopping. He hadn't mentioned they would be flying to Paris in his personal jet.

They'd left her dog at the hotel. Sam had reassured her that his assistant—Parrington—would take care of Muffin's walks, food and water. Muffin would be happier playing, after all, rather than being carted around in her carrier all day.

He was right. Besides, juggling the little crate and her packages could be tough. She'd bought so much, they'd already left a load in their chauffeured car. She hadn't had time to do any Christmas shopping with the hectic prerelease publicity schedule for *Honor*. She'd certainly fixed that problem now.

Somewhere around the fourth store, her anger at Sam for interfering had diminished to mere irritation. She didn't totally trust him. After all, what man actually wanted to go shopping? Yet he hadn't made even one move on her since they'd left the hotel. She would simply keep a wary eye on him.

A guitarist in the corner crooned "The First Noel" in French while Bella sipped her black coffee contentedly, eyeing the rest of her dessert and wondering if she dared pack on more calories. The answer? Definitely. The *poire au chocolat*—a Bosc pear, cooked in wine, dipped in chocolate, served with whipped cream—was irresistible.

She speared another bite, as the couple at the next table left, speaking in French at the speed of light.

"I'm never going to fit into my dress for the movie premiere if I let you keep feeding me like this."

He cocked a brow. "You look fabulous and you know it. Quit fishing for compliments."

"Ouch." Her irritation sparked higher. "That wasn't very nice."

Of course, most people had no way of knowing how hard an actress had to fight to stay competitive in an absurdly weight-conscious business. Bella had never been one of those stars accused of being anorexic, after all, she liked her food. But to remain in an industry where she was photographed constantly, she had to be extremely disciplined. One day, when she'd had enough of Hollywood, she planned to celebrate with a ten-day doughnut spree. All doughnuts. All the time.

He toasted her with his coffee, the bone china absurdly delicate in his large hand. "I'm a no B.S. kind of guy."

"I guess there's honor in that." She forced down miffed feelings and savored another bite, her eyes closing in ecstasy. "I love food, but it's true what they say about the camera adding pounds. I work out a lot. I decided early on I would not spend my life living on rice cakes and cocaine."

"Admirable." He seemed surprised, darn him. "Did your personal trainer come along?"

She snorted and quickly dabbed her lips with her napkin. "Don't have one. Sure I consult with trainers on how to target problem areas, but honestly, I have such a large entourage following me around with a camera documenting everything I do, I prefer to exercise alone. Well, except for Muffin of course. Muffin needs lots of exercise too or she misbehaves. So when I walk on the treadmill, she runs circles around me. I enjoy bike rides and she trots alongside. If she gives out, I have a carrier attached to the back of the seat...."

She paused mid-ramble and stared across the table at Sam who was watching her intensely. The sunset through the window cast shadows on his leanly handsome face. Had he truly been listening or was he a B.S. artist after all? Because she truly didn't have a clue why he'd signed on for a shopping trip today. Most men would have avoided this like the plague.

Bella ducked closer to him, careful to keep her voice low so the waiter angling past wouldn't overhear. "Why are we doing this? What do you hope to gain?"

"I enjoyed last night," he said simply. "I don't see why it has to be a one-time deal."

She'd been wondering, half expecting this all day, but hadn't wanted to face the inevitable discussion. Spending time with him had been more fun—laid back and easy—than she'd expected.

Now that was coming to an end. "Weren't you listening to me when I poured my heart out to you over supper? My life is a mess. I'm not in any shape for a relationship."

She wasn't in any shape to withstand more hurt.

"I never said I wanted a relationship." He set his

coffee back on the small café table and leaned on his elbow, closer, intent. "No offense meant, but I am most definitely not looking to marry you."

She leaned back, her cheeks puffing out a sigh that played with the flickering candle in the middle of their table. "Wow, no need to soft soap it."

"You're the one who asked for reassurance."

She was mad at herself even more than at him. She resented the pull of attraction even as she seemed unable to back away. "I didn't ask for anything except a change of clothes to get back to my room. You don't seem to understand." She struggled for the right words. "I am hurting, really hurting. Despite how it seemed last night, I'm not the casual-sex sort. What we did was…an anomaly."

"Stupid me." He grinned. "I thought we ate strawberries off each others' bodies."

She slapped her napkin on the table. "Quit trying to make me laugh."

"Why? You just said again how much you're hurting. Is it so wrong of me to want to make you smile?"

"As long as I still have my clothes on." Was that possible around him? Even with her defenses on full-scale alert, she couldn't help but notice the ripple of muscle under his shirt as he'd carried her packages.

Or how the appealing scruff of his five-o'clock shadow along his jaw gave him an edgier, sexy appeal. She itched to test the texture beneath her fingertips.

Against her better judgment, her fingers began crawling across the table. The very small table.

Another couple of inches and she would throw caution to the wind—

Snap, snap.

The unmistakable click of cameras sounded behind her. Damn it. Her stomach clenched in frustration—and disappointment.

Sam's face hardened. "Head down."

So far the photographer had yet to get in front of her. Sam pitched cash on the table and looped his arm around Bella's shoulders. She ducked into the strength of his protective embrace. Luckily, they'd already stored all their shopping bags in the car, so they were unencumbered to make a break for it.

He raced straight toward the restaurant's kitchen door, hurrying her alongside while shielding her face. They pushed through the double swinging doors, steam blasting through carrying the scent of frying meats. Pots clanged loudly as voices shouted instructions back and forth. A humidity-limp plaid Christmas bow hung over the clock marking six o'clock.

Sam pointed across the crowded kitchen, past the cooking island down the middle. "The back exit is that way."

"Our coats?" The winter temperatures felt all the colder to her after a lifetime in sunny California.

"Already taken care of." He rushed her past a chef in a tall white hat, the industrial stove sizzling with sliced vegetables.

An attendant stood by the back door, their coats draped over his arms. Sam had obviously made contingency plans for evading the press. She had to admire his thoroughness.

"*Merci.*" Sam shrugged into his black coat while their accomplice helped Bella with her longer one of white wool.

He shuttled her out into the empty back lot, the crisp air echoing with cathedral bells chiming "Silent Night." The lot was very empty other than their waiting transportation, thank goodness.

Sam's arm around her shoulders, he sprinted toward the Mercedes parked nearby, exhaust chugging into the early evening. "Hurry up, Cinderella, before this sucker changes into a pumpkin."

The chauffer swept open the door. Bella slid in as Sam launched into the other side. Her heart pounded from the exertion as much as the threat. She knew too well how quickly a frenzy of reporters could cause an accident by jumping all over a car. Once their car pulled out onto the main road, two motorcycles roared away from the curb.

The press had found them.

Their driver raced through the streets of Paris at a breakneck speed, motorcycles speeding closer behind. Her pulse thudding in her ears, Bella double-checked her seat belt. Sam pulled out his cell phone, issuing instructions for the crew on his plane to be ready for takeoff. Otherwise, silence hovered heavily in the vehicle as she checked anxiously over her shoulder.

Mere minutes later, they pulled into the small

private airport, through a security gate. Sam's silver private jet waited, the crew prepped and ready outside.

She leaped from the vehicle. A few yards away, the paparazzi on motorcycles screeched to a halt behind the fence. They wouldn't get any farther, but their cameras had mighty powerful lenses.

"Hurry!" He ushered her up the airplane steps. "That security guard isn't going to hold up much longer."

Two men wearing vests with reflective tape unloaded her packages from the trunk at lightning speed while she raced up the metal stairs.

Inside, she unlooped her scarf and sunk into the leather seat. Gasping for air, she couldn't recall feeling this breathless in a long time. She should have been frustrated, angry even.

Yet for some reason it had felt more like an adventure with Sam at her side.

Because she'd never doubted he would take care of the situation? "I can't believe you managed to elude them all day."

Sam sidestepped the media center dominating most of the space. He secured his seat belt near the wine refrigerator at an old-fashioned bar. Sparkling cut-crystal glasses hung upside down above a black, granite prep area. "It helps that you speak fluent French when shopping or ordering meals."

"As do you."

His fluency in the language shouldn't have surprised her since he worked here, but it did make her wonder what other surprises he had in store.

"People see what they expect to see. We appeared to be two locals finishing up last-minute Christmas shopping."

Still, Sam had a knack for ditching the press beyond anything she'd seen before. And given the high-profile Hollywood sorts who made up her regular circle, she'd seen some mighty adept press dodgers.

The airplane engines roared louder, the craft easing forward, faster, until the nose lifted off. With a smooth swoop they were airborne. The neat pile of her shopping bags barely moved from where they rested in a corner.

And it was quite a hefty pile.

She'd checked off everyone on her growing list of family members. Buying for her grandmother had been particularly difficult—and sad. What did you get for a person who wasn't expected to live much longer?

She hoped she'd chosen well.

God, what was she even thinking wasting her grandmother's final precious days apart? Or worse yet, what if her grandmother died before Bella could say goodbye?

The holiday cheer she'd found with Sam seeped away. Even the twinkling lights of the Eiffel Tower were fading in the distance. Her escape was truly over. Time to face reality—and Beverly Hills—again.

She needed to tell Sam that while their day shopping together had been special, come morning, she would be leaving for California.

* * *

Sam could see Bella mentally pulling away from him as clearly as if she'd risen from her seat and hopped out of the plane.

He wasn't sure what had changed, but most certainly he'd lost some ground. He needed to get her talking again so he could find the right opening. No great hardship, actually. Spending time with her today—even out of bed—had been surprisingly entertaining.

She hadn't shopped like a diva with the world at her feet. There hadn't been any special requests for private showings or traipsing up the aisles with complimentary champagne in hand. Bella spent most of her time admiring the different style crèches, delighting in everything from delicate crystal figurines to rustic wood carvings. She'd slid a huge donation into a charitable collection plate when she thought he wasn't looking, then turned around and purchased a miniature *père Noël* bell on a ribbon to drape around her neck—his own personal Christmas elf.

The tinkling of that small bell had charmed and seduced him all day long.

She was a total turn-on even totally clothed.

Bella shifted in her seat, her green silk blouse inching open to flash him a hint of creamy skin. "Thanks for helping me with my shopping," she said, jump-starting the conversation for him. "This worked out perfectly since I really do have to get back home tomorrow."

Damn. Time was shorter than he'd anticipated, but lucky for him, he already had business dealings lined up in California, the most recent in Los Angeles. He could combine work and pleasure quite easily.

He just needed the right opening to suggest a visit to her side of the Atlantic. "And where exactly is home for you?"

"At the family estate on Loma Vista Drive in Beverly Hills. I stay in the guesthouse." Her brow puckered. "Where do you actually live?"

A promising move that she asked more about him. Sam stretched his legs in front of him as the plane droned through the dark sky. "Most of the family is located in southern Florida, but Garrison hotels have been expanding of late. I've taken on more traveling responsibilities as many of my family members are marrying and settling down. I oversee most new projects in the works."

"But where do you *live*?" she asked again as she propped her chin on her hand.

"In my hotels." Everything was provided for him. Why bother keeping a condo or home that would leave him losing valuable work hours commuting?

"The epitome of a rootless bachelor."

"That would be me. A no-commitment guy. No worries about me leading you on." The truth should put her at ease.

Studying him, Bella twisted a lock of hair then stopped abruptly as if realizing how damn sexy she looked with that simple gesture. "I don't want you to get the wrong idea."

"What idea would that be?"

"The sex was amazing, no question." She chewed her bottom lip for a blood surging second that threatened to send him reaching for her again. "But I'm not interested in any kind of relationship, even a no-strings fling."

"Who said I am?"

"Then what are we doing here?" She gestured between them.

"I'm making restitution for the inconvenience caused by my hotel's security lapse. My business is everything to me." Now to start easing into his plan for more time to win her over. "In fact, I have a new hotel opening in the U.S. I would have been heading back to the States soon to check on the progress anyway."

"You take your commitment to your guests above and beyond." She eyed him suspiciously. "Where is the new hotel?"

"Los Angeles, actually." True enough. The hotel was almost ready to open as the latest in Garrison Grande Incorporated's successful expansion plan.

Her brows pinched together. "Yeah, right. You just happen to have a hotel in the town where I live," she said suspiciously. "Where in Los Angeles?"

He recited the address, a piece of prime property he'd busted his ass negotiating for.

Her eyes went wide. "You really do have a hotel there?"

"Bella, it's not like I could or would lie about this. It's easy enough to check out."

"Of course. I'm sorry." The defensiveness eased from her shoulders and she relaxed back in the white leather seat. "I'm just not sure what to think of you yet. You've been so nice, but then you went behind my back to call Charlotte, albeit with seemingly good intentions."

She shoved her hand through her wind-tumbled red hair. "I just don't know what to think these days. I'm probably being prickly and a little paranoid. I'm nervous about going back and facing everyone again at the premiere of *Honor*. It's difficult enough dealing with Grandmere's cancer. I'll also have to face my parents and pretend I'm okay with everything." She exhaled long, her cheeks puffing. "Then of course Ridley will be there."

Ridley the Rat? Jealousy kicked around inside his gut. Sam stroked his jaw. "I imagine seeing him at the premiere will be tough."

She pressed her hands to her forehead. "I don't even want to think about it. Which makes me mad at him all over again. The premiere of *Honor* on Christmas day should be one of the best days of my life and he's wrecking it. He'll show up with his new bimbo girlfriend and I'll be there with my dog."

He leaned toward her. "Use me."

Her hands fell to her lap. "What?"

The more he thought about it, the more it made sense. He'd been looking for an opening and she'd just handed him the ideal opportunity. "Take me as your date to the premiere. Use me to show that loser ex-boyfriend of yours that you aren't shedding any tears over him. At the risk of sounding as if I have an overinflated ego, magazines seem to think I'm a fairly eligible bachelor."

"So I've seen." She toyed with the thin velvet ribbon around her neck, nudging the small bell just above the top button on her blouse. A hell of a distraction for his eyes. "But *use* you? Wouldn't that be shallow of me?"

"Not if we're both in agreement."

"What do you gain from this?"

Bella back in his bed?

But a smart man would lead with another argument and no one had ever called him a fool. "For starters, I get to take a breather from appearing on all those damn 'most eligible bachelor' lists. Every time they publish one, a fresh flock of matchmaking mamas shows up at one of my hotels. It's insulting to me and to their daughters. Not to mention a real pain in the ass."

"Okay, I can understand that." She nodded slowly. "I have to leave tomorrow."

"Not a problem." He only slept for a few hours anyway. He could wrap up business and be ready by sunup. He'd been planning a trip later next week after Christmas anyhow. "Any other questions?"

"Yeah," she said empathically, "a big one. Why me?"

"Because I can be honest with you about this and know you're not going to run to the press."

She smiled grudgingly. "You have me there."

"You agree?" That easily. Hot damn. Peeling her clothes off her after that premiere would make for a night to remember. He would pleasure her so thoroughly he would wipe Ridley Sinclair from her memory forever.

"We're not sleeping together again."

"Seems like you're cutting your nose off to spite your face with that one." He held up a hand to stop her protest. He knew to quit when he was ahead, and he'd definitely taken a huge step ahead in getting her to agree to let him hang out with her over the holidays. "But, hell, who am I to judge? No sex. We'll leave first thing tomorrow morning. Agreed?"

She hesitated only a moment, frowning briefly before her face cleared. "I have the feeling I'm going to regret this…but…yes. We'll go to the Christmas-day premiere together."

Six

As Bella sat on Sam's plane the next morning on her way back to the States, she couldn't believe she'd actually said yes to his outrageous proposition.

Petting Muffin in her lap, Bella stared out the window at the Atlantic Ocean peeking below while the plane zipped in and out of clouds. Footsteps echoed as Sam walked to the front of the plane, toward the kitchenette for a snack, his long legs eating up the space in only a few strides.

She knew one thing for sure. Sam was a damn good businessman. He'd presented the case well for sticking together awhile longer, knowing right where she was most vulnerable. Her pride stung at the thought of facing Ridley alone.

Yet Sam *had* agreed to her no sex stipulation.

Her gaze dipped to his fine tush showcased in casual blue pants. In a weak moment she wondered what he would look like filling out a pair of well-washed jeans?

She shook off the too-enticing fantasy. She'd meant what she'd said about no sex, especially not now when she was so confused and, well, weak when it came to his appeal. She wasn't one for flings, in fact didn't have much of a dating past other than Ridley because of her drive to break out in her career.

Had Sam been lying about keeping his distance, or was he really genuine about seeing benefits in helping her out? Maybe he was just one of those gallant guys who couldn't resist a woman in distress.

After the way his mother had been treated, Bella could understand how he would have developed that tendency. Maybe he didn't really have a hidden agenda. Perhaps he genuinely had business to accomplish and figured he would be a good guy along the way.

Her initial idea for facing Ridley at the premiere had been to borrow one of her brothers for the evening. But how lame was that? Sam would make for a powerful piece of eye candy to distract gossip-hungry people from wondering why she and Ridley were no longer an item.

She could ruminate about this all morning, but regardless, her escape to France was officially over. She couldn't hide from her family's drama anymore. Thanks to Sam, she wouldn't be facing everyone alone.

Bella sagged back in her seat, sliding the shade closed over the small oval airplane window. She scrubbed her fists along her gritty eyes. She hadn't slept well, tossing and turning all night as she worried if she'd made the right choice in coming back to the States with Sam. A yawn stretched her face.

The bed behind the privacy door was inviting, but she feared sending the wrong message. Hell, she feared her own willpower weakening if she crawled onto a mattress with Sam anywhere near. She was better off making use of the additional sleeper chairs out here.

Was she cutting off her nose to spite her face, as he'd said?

No, damn it. She wasn't in any position for a new relationship. It wouldn't be fair to him or to her.

Caffeine, yeah, that was the ticket. She just needed more caffeine to jolt her awake and get her brain working again.

She unbuckled her lap belt, placed sleeping Muffin on the seat and strode forward to the small kitchen area where Sam had headed a few minutes earlier. "Anything with caffeine up here?"

Sam's back tensed at her words, his shoulders rising ever so slightly. He shoved his hands in his pants pockets and turned toward her. "Coffee, tea, soda, your choice. Let me know and I'll pour it for you. The steward is up with the pilot right now."

"I can serve myself." She sidled by him in the

narrow galley kitchen. Very narrow. The heat of his body permeated through her thin blouse, his chest grazing her breasts. "What are you having?"

"Just bottled water." He angled past and out of her way, even as his silvery-gray gaze stayed locked in tight on her.

Bella opened the stainless-steel mini-refrigerator and pulled out a Diet Coke from the rows of neatly arranged beverages, fresh fruits and cheeses inside. She considered fishing through the dark mahogany cabinets for a cup and ice, but her hands had started shaking right about the time his body had rubbed ever so enticingly against hers. She wrapped a napkin around the can and popped the top.

A bracing gulp later, she worked to establish some emotional distance again. "I appreciate your help with the Ridley issue, but I want to make sure you understand. No more interfering with my family like you did by calling Charlotte's husband."

"Wouldn't dream of it."

"You're lying."

He leaned against the bulkhead, his feet crossed in front of him. The sun glinted through the oval window highlighting hints of russet in his deep brown hair. "You sure are a charmer today, Bella." He smiled wide and wicked. "Why would you accuse me of something so devious?"

She wadded her napkin and tossed it at his chest. "Because you have a reputation for being ruthless when you want your way."

Beyond his success in the work world, she'd heard rumors he changed women with the season.

"I make no secret of being a driven, determined person." He cocked an eyebrow. "Of course that could mean you're reckless in climbing onto my airplane."

"Ha-ha. Not amused." She passed him his bottled water. "If we're going to give this 'friends' thing an honest go, then you need to be truthful with me."

Sam stiffened, only a hint and only for a second, but enough to make her wonder what he was covering up.

He reached for his drink, taking it with his left hand, rather than his right, which he kept stuffed in his pocket.

Like he was hiding something.

She thought back to when she'd come to the galley. He'd only been drinking water. What else could he have…

An awful, awful possibility—probability—flooded her mind. She'd seen the look and stance often enough when walking in on people at inopportune times at parties or raves.

Oh, my God. Sam was hiding more than she'd thought, something she never would have considered. "What were you doing here before I walked up?"

"Getting a drink of water, like I said." His face went totally blank.

His complete lack of expression spoke louder than anything else. He should have been at ease.

She planted her hands on her hips. "Like hell. I've

been around Hollywood types all my life. I've seen more than my share of alcohol and drug abuse." Disillusionment threatened to swamp her even as her anger topped the charts. "You're popping pills."

His jaw dropped open for a flash, then snapped shut.

But he didn't deny it.

She stood her ground. She might be hurt, but she was also mad as hell and she wasn't backing down. "I may have to put up with that kind of behavior from those I work with, but I absolutely will not tolerate it in my private life."

His frozen face cleared and…he laughed. Not just a chuckle, but head-back, full-out laughter that muffled even the drone of the airplane engines. Was that what his drugs did for him? Separate him from reality so thoroughly he found this amusing?

Steam built inside her, fuming, filling her with anger and cynicism. That made her all the madder. She shouldn't care what kind of man he was. He should mean nothing to her.

But this disappointment on top of everything else was just too much. "Don't you *dare* mock me. I'm serious. Get out. Get out now."

He scratched his forehead. "I'm afraid I can't accommodate you there. We're in the air, in *my* plane."

She stomped her foot. "Damn it, you make me so mad sometimes."

His laughter faded, but his grin remained. "Good God, you're even hotter when you're fired up."

His eyes sparked with awareness, his gaze locking

on her face so long she suddenly felt self-conscious. "I'll just go back to my seat."

She started to turn and he caught her arm. The heat of his familiar touch seared through her lightweight sweater. He stared down at her with somber gray eyes. "I'm not popping illegal drugs."

He pulled his other hand out of his pocket, a pill bottle in palm.

She shoved his wrist away. "Prescription drugs, then. Abuse and addiction all the same. Go get high somewhere else."

He thrust his hand forward insistently. "Look at the label."

She frowned. "The label?"

"I'm taking allergy medicine."

Oh crap. She'd let her temper take control and screwed up. She owed him a whopper of an apology. "You have allergies?"

"I am a human being, last time I checked anyway." He held up the bottle and rattled the pills. "Humans get sick."

"What are you allergic to?" Unease prickled up her spine with an impending sense of doom as she crossed her fingers, hoping he wouldn't say what she feared.

He dropped the bottle of allergy meds back in his pocket and faced her straight on. "I'm allergic to dogs."

Ah hell.
His secret was out.

He'd done a decent job at hiding his allergy to her dog before, popping pills and trying to put distance between himself and the mutt. Their shopping jaunt in Paris—with Muffin staying back at the hotel—had given his sinuses a break. But the recycled air in the plane was really wreaking havoc with his allergies.

He hated weakness, any lack of control over his mind or his body. Ever since his mother had brought home a chocolate Lab puppy for his seventh birthday he'd known extended exposure to dogs made his sinuses go haywire.

Bella's hand floated to her chest, over her heart. "You took allergy pills so you could be with me?"

Her blue eyes glinted with a wonder that made him itchy. "Vanity dogs are a must for a large number of my clientele. So the hotel allows small pets."

True enough, but the passing contact wasn't enough to cause a problem. Still, she didn't know he'd put the call in to his doctor for the meds just so he could be near Bella—and Muffin.

Her look of wonder faded to irritation, her chest heaving with indignation. "Vanity pets? *Vanity* pets! Muffin is *not* a vanity pet."

"Well of course not," he said, unable to peel his eyes off the flush spreading along her milky skin. "That is not one of those purebred, froufrou animals."

Bella relaxed and started swiping a few stray dog hairs off her black jeans.

He couldn't resist needling her. "She's too damn ugly to be a vanity pet."

"Ugly?" she gasped, her hands fisting. "I cannot believe you just called my precious Muffin ugly."

The door leading to the cockpit creaked open.... Then closed again as the folks up front must have realized no one was in danger.

Damn, Bella was hot when she got all fired up, which led him to keep right on stoking the flames. "Good God, have you checked out your dog's Billy Idol snarl lately?"

"Shush!" She glanced back at the sleeping dog as if somehow the animal might understand his words. "She's a sweetie pie."

"I never said she wasn't—"

"Last time I checked—" she staked closer, jabbing a finger in his chest "—it's the inside that counts, not appearance. If I turned ugly tomorrow, would you stop being my friend?"

"We're friends?" That was a start.

"We *were*."

Were? Past tense? Not so fast, Bella. He advanced a step, pushing his chest against her poking pointer finger. "So you consider yourself beautiful."

She snatched her hand back and crossed her arms. "I don't consider myself vain. Understanding strengths and weaknesses is a part of the business."

Something niggled at him about her reasoning. "Am I to assume you believe you're only chosen for roles because of your looks?"

"I want to be taken seriously as an actress. That's why I fought so hard to get the lead in this film." Her fists unfurled and she studied her nails. "My brothers were always the brains in the family."

He thought of a thousand ways she'd shown her innate intelligence in the short time he'd known her—her knowledge of French architecture while they'd been shopping. Her quick wit. He could think of a number of other examples, but he suspected she would just brush those aside in embarrassment.

What a strange dichotomy she presented. One of America's hottest women was a mass of insecurities.

Since he couldn't tell her what he really wanted to—that she was so damn hot and smart he wanted to take her behind that curtain and tangle up with her on the bed until they landed in the States—he opted for, "I'm sorry for saying your dog is ugly."

Muffin perked up in the leather chair, her ears twitched. Damned if that mutt actually could understand humans.

The dog jumped to the ground and scampered to her owner. Bella scooped her up and snuggled her scruffy pet under her chin. "Muffin forgives you. But it may take *me* a little while longer."

"For what it's worth, I think Billy Idol is a badass." He winked, stroking a finger along Muffin's chin, then Bella's.

She froze.

Her chest rose and fell faster, her lips parting with each gusty breath. Memories of their night together flared to life in his mind until he could taste her, feel her even without touching. He was right to link up with her this way. They both deserved more of what they'd shared in his suite. He wouldn't let her be so foolish as to throw away a chance at enjoying the chemistry between them until it ran its course.

He stroked her cheek with his knuckles. When she didn't twitch away, he leaned toward her, already anticipating the explosion of sensation that would come just from sealing his mouth to hers—

The PA crackled to life. "Mr. Garrison," the pilot's voice called over the speaker, "we're heading into some turbulence. You will both need to buckle into your seats, please."

Bella blinked fast, clutched her dog closer and angled past him double-time without a word. Her silence and evasive eyes were all the more telling than any words of dismissal.

All talk of friendship and no sex be damned, she wanted him, too. Now he just needed to show some restraint until that desire grew so taut *she* came to *him*.

Bella stood on her front stoop with Sam as the sun hovered low on the horizon. While it was only suppertime in California, she was suffering from a serious case of jet lag. A car's motor sounded in the distance but continued around the drive toward Hudson Manor's twelve-car parking garage.

Sam pressed a hand to the door frame, stopping her from passing. "So this is your place."

She leaned against the railing, not as eager to leave as she would have expected. The whole allergy pills incident still whirled around in her head. He may not have taken the meds just for her, but he was continuing to do so because of Muffin and that tugged at her heart.

Beyond that, she was relieved to see his unmistakable disapproval of drugs. She'd witnessed firsthand the ruin too much money could bring to people who snorted their wealth up their noses. "I moved here to the guesthouse a few years ago to live on my own. Of course it's obvious I didn't move too far away from my relatives."

She'd made her big independent stand by moving across the lawn and redecorating the two-bedroom, one-story cottage in a shabby chic, Bohemian style totally at odds with the French Provincial formality of Hudson Manor.

She'd needed to step out of her very large family's shadow, find her own style and voice. Right after moving in, she'd painted each room according to different moods. Blue ceilings to evoke the sky. Green-painted hardwood floors with sea-grass mats to ground her in the natural world. Her bedroom ceiling was dotted with stars. She'd even used a constellation map for accuracy but regretted that the night sky was permanently set to October. She made a home for herself rather than letting some decorator stamp his own personality onto her life.

Security lights flickered on as the sun drifted deeper into the horizon. Her childhood house loomed in the distance, a fifty-five-room white stone and wrought-iron mansion. Fifteen acres of sculpted landscape afforded plenty of privacy here.

Privacy with her whole big family all around. She eyed the lengthy garage in the distance and all the doors were closed. She tucked deeper onto the porch so a sprawling tree would block them from any curious eyes in the main house.

She stared up into Sam's mesmerizing gray eyes, allowing herself a moment to just sink into their appeal. "Thank you."

"For what?"

"For bringing me home, for the shopping trip in Paris, for clotheslining the reporter, for offering to come with me to the premiere, for taking allergy pills." She stared down, scuffing her red heels along the stone step. "For respecting my stance on no more sex."

"I respect your opinion, but make no mistake, that doesn't mean I agree."

She pressed a hand to his chest, his really hard and hot chest. "Hey, I mean it when I say I'm not going to invite you inside, not even for coffee."

"I'm a man who stands by his word." He picked up her hand and linked their fingers. "As much as I detest media attention, maybe if I feed the hungry press hounds for a few days they might get off my back."

Since she intended to be an actress for as long as the industry would hire her, her life would be full of media frenzy indefinitely. Sam had made his feelings about the press known. Sure she wanted privacy at times, but she also appreciated the hand they played in helping her promote her work.

That put her lifestyle in direct conflict to his. She didn't have to worry about him pressing for more. His short-term offer must be as genuine as it sounded.

Great news.

Right?

So why did it leave her wanting to squeeze his hand, yank him closer and steal up all the kisses she possibly could?

Her mouth dried and she forced herself not to moisten her lips. "Good luck with your new hotel."

A hotel nearby in Los Angeles. A hotel that could bring him back again in the future…. She stopped those thoughts short.

"Luck? Hard work makes luck more inevitable."

"I like that." She was actually finding she liked *him* and that was a dangerous thought to have while standing on her front stoop. Too easily this man could entice her to toss aside her intentions to keep him— any man—at arm's length until her life settled back down again. "I spend a lot of time with diva sorts, male and female, who barely carry their own bottled water, much less a suitcase."

Damn him for being so muscular and charming and enticing. What would it have been like to meet him before she'd made the mistake of falling for Ridley? Back during a time when she'd believed her parents had the perfect marriage and happily ever after was for real.

She would have invited Sam into her home, into her bed.

He leaned toward her as he'd done on the airplane. She'd wanted him then, wanted him even more now, a need made all the more painful because she knew just how good they could be together. Her body flamed in response, memories of champagne kisses still fresh in her mind. He angled closer—to open her door.

Sam placed her suitcase in the entryway and set Muffin's carrier alongside.

"Goodnight, Bella." He backed a step, waving once before turning toward the limousine. "I'll be in touch."

Touch. She shivered with want. It was going to be a long night.

Seven

Sam sprawled on the backstage studio sofa watching the television screen in the green room while Bella finished an interview on the *Tonight Show*. Muffin perched on her lap, wearing a plaid Christmas sweater. The mutt actually quietly behaved for the cameras as Bella encouraged viewers to rescue a pet from the pound for the holidays.

God, she looked hot in a frothy green dress, silver sequins belting it just below her breasts. Her hair flowed over her shoulders in a deliberate disarray that spoke of steamy, out-of-control sex.

He'd seen just that hair style on her—for real.

Sam shifted uncomfortably. He'd kept his distance up to now, restricting contact to phone calls. She didn't even know he was here at the Christmas Eve taping, but he figured this would be a great time to start rumors flying about the two of them before they showed up together at tomorrow's premiere.

A network intern refilled the water glass beside him. He nodded his thanks to the young woman, but kept his eyes firmly planted on the television screen.

Bella had spent the past two days doing interviews while he'd attended to business at his hotel. He'd given her space, easy enough to manage with their movie premiere date just around the corner. He'd seen the want in her eyes on her front stoop the night they'd arrived in the States. A couple of days to ponder that and let it grow could be a good thing.

Except that it had backfired by ramping up his desire for her as well.

Sam knocked back half his tonic water and studied the interview in progress. Framed by the TV screen, Bella smiled flirtatiously at the talk-show host, her hand fluttering to rest on his arm.

The talk-show host loosened his tie in a moment that made the audience laugh. Sam wasn't chuckling. The NFL quarterback sitting on her other side— having finished his interview—hadn't taken his damn eyes off her plunging neckline since he'd risen to hug her too tightly when she'd walked across the stage.

Sam bit back a curse. He understood the PR game. Bella wasn't Tiffany. And even if Bella's inviting smile and batting eyelashes were genuine she'd made it clear Sam had no claim to her.

The host leaned closer across his desk, L.A. skyline superimposed behind them. "What's the deal with you and your costar Ridley Sinclair? You two were a couple and now I hear there's another guy in the green room waiting for you."

Bella stroked her dog with undue attention as if stalling to gather her thoughts. "You've been checking out the green room?"

The camera shot shifted to a split screen image of her—and of him. Damn. He'd meant to surprise her, but not this way.

Making it all the more awkward, the camera angle had included a vase full of red roses interspersed with holly sprigs. The flowers were all over the back-stage area as part of the holiday decorations, but the audience didn't know that. It looked as if he'd brought the bouquet for Bella.

Not a bad idea, if he'd thought of it, but he had gift plans of his own for tomorrow. He shot a laid-back smile and wave to the camera, stifling an itch at the media attention.

To her credit, Bella recovered quickly. "Hi, Sam." She blew him a flirty little kiss. "Thanks for the flowers."

Muffin raised her head and yipped.

The host grinned and—thank God—the screen returned to the regular image of the stage. "Tell us more about this new man in your life, Sam Garrison. I understand he is the owner of a string of Garrison Grande hotels."

Bella stroked Muffin in a gesture Sam had come to recognize as self-soothing. "Sam owns the Garrison Grande Marseille near where we filmed parts of the movie and he has a new hotel here in L.A. We'd planned to spring the news at the premiere tomorrow—" her mouth tightened slightly "—but you've found us out."

"What about you and Ridley Sinclair?" the host pressed.

"Ridley and I—" she waved a dismissive hand and laughed lightly "—went out a few times while making the movie, nothing more. I'm afraid the PR people may have gone a little overboard with all those joint publicity shots and, so, that's how rumors start. What can I say? It played well for the film."

"Ah, could you have been leading us on all the time with the Ridley rumors in order to hide your other relationship in the works?"

She batted her eyelashes. "Now would I mislead the press like that?"

The audience rumbled with laughter.

Damn, she was good at maneuvering people into believing her time with Ridley was nothing more than a couple of shared hamburgers. Yet, she'd never once lied in any of her answers to the talk-show host.

The interview was wrapping up and soon enough he would see Bella, another brief brush to remind her of the chemistry they shared simply by standing in the same room. She probably had Christmas Eve plans anyway and he wasn't much for holidays. His mother had ventured out to spend a week with her

South Beach relatives, and he had work to clear away if he intended to devote all of tomorrow to Bella's premiere and post gala.

The green room door opened and Sam rose to his feet, a surge of excitement just over seeing Bella knocking him a little off guard.

Except it wasn't Bella. Rather, an older man walked in, slickly dressed, wearing an ostentatious ascot. The guy looked vaguely familiar, but Sam couldn't quite place him.

Medium height, dark hair, probably around fifty, and he had a Hollywood smile. This fella was definitely a part of the industry.

The man made a beeline for the intern with a clipboard. "Hello, lovely lady, I hope you can help me."

The assistant giggled, sidling closer. "Yes, sir? What can I do for you?"

"I'm here to check up on the star of my film— Bella Hudson."

"Your film?" Her eyes went star-struck wide.

"I'm the director of *Honor*." He thrust out his hand. "I'm David Hudson."

Anger pumped through Sam at the man who'd betrayed and dishonored his family. A man who'd knocked a spirited woman like Bella off-kilter. Something Sam intended to make sure it didn't happen again tonight.

Bella secured her hold on Muffin's short leash and rushed down the busy hall toward the green room.

She tucked sideways past a line of pet trainers waiting their turn for an interview. Muffin growled at the snake handler with his mammoth reptile curled in a cage.

Ewww.

Skin crawling, she focused her eyes forward, past signed and framed photos of prior guests with the host, toward the door at the end of the hall. Where Sam waited for *her*. How sweet that he'd showed up in support. They'd spoken on the phone since returning to the States, but hadn't planned to see each other until the Christmas premiere.

Her stomach fluttered, catching her unaware. Viewing him on that studio screen shouldn't affect her this much. Yet still she doubled-timed down the corridor.

Pausing outside the door, she fluffed her hair with her nails, checked the string straps of her seafoam dress, and smoothed the flirty hem down to where it stopped just above her knees. Muffin danced around her legs in protest over having the leash tugged.

Bella glanced down. "Sorry, precious."

Damn. How many times had she asserted to Sam that looks didn't matter? She forced her arms back to her sides, shaking out her hands to release nerves.

Deep breath. She strode slowly through the door as if in no hurry at all, Muffin trotting alongside. A girl with a clipboard stood by the refreshments cart, jotting notes beside the empty sofa where Sam had been sitting. Bella twirled, looked around, but the room was otherwise vacant.

She walked over to the young intern taking stock of the coffee supply. "Excuse me?"

The intern spun to face her, pageboy haircut swishing in her enthusiasm. "Yes, Ms. Hudson. Can I help you with something?"

Bella waved toward the sofa where the video screen had showed Sam earlier. "What happened to the man who was waiting back here?"

"Which one?" She clutched the clipboard to her chest. "The younger hunk or the older charmer?"

"The young hunk, without question," she answered, surprised at the hint of territorialism that crept into her voice.

"He left with the older gentleman."

"Oh." Disappointment stabbed. Had he met up with a friend? Or brought along a business acquaintance, merely stopping in for her PR on his way to something else? He'd made it clear more than once that his work came first. She couldn't resist asking, "Any idea who was with him?"

The star-struck intern's eyes gleamed with excitement. "I sure do. Mr. Garrison was with the director of your movie."

Ah crap. She grabbed the edge of the sofa to bolster her suddenly wobbly knees.

Uncle David. Not her uncle. Her real father. Had come here. No. No. No.

Her heart thudded hard in her chest, darn near thumping to her stomach. She accepted she would have to face him at the premiere, but that should be hectic enough for her to be able to stay away from him. She wasn't ready for a face-to-face, especially a surprise meeting. Not yet. Maybe never.

What if she'd seen him, now, unprepared? Her throat tightened. Had he come simply because of the movie? Of course he had. He didn't care about her any more than he cared about his other two children. The bastard.

And Sam had left with him.

Why?

Her mind churned. Sam knew how she felt about her biological father. He could only have lured David away to spare her the stress of an unexpected visit. It was thoughtful, and yes, even helpful, but... She couldn't help but think how he'd interfered again, much as he'd done with Charlotte.

God, he confused her, thoughtful but pushy.

And he took allergy pills to be near Muffin.

Bella flopped on the sofa beside the vase of roses speckled with holly. Disappointment over not seeing Sam pinched harder than her silver Ferragamo heels.

Harder than she would have expected given she'd known the man less than a week.

She was a total mess, in no way ready to deal with complicated relationships. And she doubted her mind would be any more settled by the time she saw Sam at the Christmas premiere.

Bella couldn't imagine a Christmas more exciting—and tumultuous—than this one.

Sitting in her unabashedly frilly bedroom retreat with a hairdresser working behind her and a friend beside her gabbing away, Bella glanced at the clock. Forty-five minutes until she would leave for the opening of *Honor.*

Forty-five minutes until she would see Sam.

She hadn't even been able to speak with him after her Christmas Eve interview when he'd left with David. As much as she feared her out-of-control emotions around Sam, curiosity was eating her alive.

Along with irritation.

Bella fidgeted on the pink-paisley vanity chair as the hairstylist pinned loops of hair in place. She'd expected Sam to be more ardent in pursuing her. Maybe he'd really meant what he said about this merely being a convenient arrangement.

Damn it, she hated sitting still because it gave her too much time to think. She preferred to be moving, busy, active.

Tough to do when having her hair yanked. At least she didn't have to hang out alone. Her brother Max's fiancée Dana kept her company while Muffin snoozed in her puppy bed—a small white wrought-iron model that matched Bella's larger version across the room. The stylist worked his magic while Dana rambled on about family gossip. Dana was the one to comfort her when the news about David and her mother Sabrina's affair came out.

Dana was there for her now, already dressed for the big event in a sleek bronze dress with yellow diamond accent jewelry that complimented her olive skin and luminous dark brown eyes. Uber-efficient Dana wouldn't be a mental mess over some guy. Dana glided around the room straightening covers, tossing a discarded nightie in the hamper, straightening a stack of scripts for future projects her agent had messengered over for Bella's consideration.

The male hairstylist from Hudson Studios tapped Bella's shoulders. "Sit up straight, please."

Perched on a vanity chair in only a camisole and tap pants, she forced herself not to slump while her red hair was twisted into at least a gazillion swirls.

She cut her eyes toward Dana since she wasn't allowed to move her cramping muscles. "Thanks for hanging out with me. I would have died of boredom without you. I'm sure there are things you would rather do with your Christmas than babysit me."

Dana dropped into a floral, ruffle skirted armchair. "You're family. And besides—" she grazed her fingers over the yellow teardrop diamond resting in the V of her low-cut gown "—what woman doesn't like to be draped in a mint's worth of jewels? It's not every day I have the excuse to wear this kind of bling."

"You're a gem yourself. My brother's a lucky man." She resisted the urge to chew off her peachy lipstick. "It's kinda sad that it takes a movie premiere to bring the rest of our family together for the holidays. If nothing else, everyone should be here for Grandmere."

Even if that meant she had to put up with the

debacle between her parents and David. Would there be some kind of blowup with the three of them in one place? It sucked to think the best she could hope for was painfully thick tension. She couldn't ignore her gratitude that Sam had saved her that tension the night before.

Dana grimaced. "Umm, I guess you haven't heard via the Hudson grapevine, but while you were in France, Dev and Valerie separated."

"What?" Her oldest brother had split up with his wife? "Already? I had my doubts about them, but still, they only eloped a few months ago."

"I realize he's your brother, but you have to know he never treated Valerie very well. Maybe this will make him wake up before he loses her altogether," Dana said logically, pointing out a missed thread of hair to the stylist.

How could she keep a cool head about things like this?

Bella held still in spite of the yanking tugs on her hair. At least they didn't have to worry about the stylist spouting gossip, not if he wanted to keep his high-profile job with the studio.

Of course so far it wasn't as if she and Dana were revealing state secrets. "I'm not holding my breath on Dev scrounging up an empathy gene."

Dana crossed her legs, gold strappy high heel dangling off her toe. "What's the scoop with you and this hotel mogul?"

"It's nothing serious." Which was exactly what

she'd asked for, yet she couldn't help feeling miffed at his no-show lack of attention.

"He came all the way from France to Beverly Hills just to 'hang out' with you."

"He has business here." And he'd protected her from David. Yet hadn't so much as met her for coffee. Although that hadn't stopped her from having her driver detour by Sam's new hotel to scope out the project he had in the works—a mighty high-end impressive project.

"Business? Uh-huh. Whatever."

She wasn't sure if she wanted Dana to be right or not. "I appreciate your optimism, but I'm fairly certain long-term romance just isn't in the cards for me anytime soon." *If ever.* "Think about it. Dev broke up with his brand-new wife. My parents aren't speaking to each other. We don't even need to go into how crummy Uncle David's marriage was before Aunt Ava died. I don't mean to be a wet blanket, but how are you not shaking in your shoes over becoming a Hudson?"

Dana leaned forward. "Max and I are happy. So are Luc and Gwen." Bella's brothers, Markus's biological sons along with Dev. "And what about Charlotte and Alec? Even Jack and CeCe beat the odds and got back together again."

Jack and Charlotte—Bella's new half siblings. Good Lord, her family tree had more branches than a national savings and loan—and about as much stability.

The hairstylist held up an industrial-size bottle of hairspray. "Close your eyes, Ms. Hudson."

Bella squeezed her eyes closed as the mist of organic hair product swirled around her. "Face it, Dana. There's still plenty of time left to screw it up."

Dana sneezed. "Thanks. Keep that up and next time I'm going to sneeze on your dress."

Half a bottle later, the hairstylist put away his spritzer bottle and started packing his supplies. Bella peeked through one eye and stood. Turning her head from side to side in front of the mirror, she checked out the Grecian-inspired updo.

Dana slipped the specially crafted gown from the hanger and held it for Bella. "Okay, sweetie, time's a-wasting."

Bella turned from the mirror and stepped into the dress. She pulled the cool fabric up her body, then shimmied out of her camisole, flicking it free.

Dana zipped the dress up the back slowly. "Spin around and let us see."

The ivory velvet strapless with a beaded top—a Marchesa creation just for her—draped her curves to pool at her feet in a style somewhat reminiscent of her dash with a sheet down a hotel corridor back in France.

Except this time she had a full face of makeup and upswept hair. She wore her grandmother's diamond necklace in spite of the offers from major jewelers to display their wares. Bella placed her hand over the necklace, her rapid heartbeat thudding under her touch.

Nerves tap-danced in her stomach over how *Honor* would be received. Over her combustible family gathered in one place. Over seeing Sam when he kept her constantly off-balance. The evening could shatter into a debacle so easily.

Dana clapped her hands. "Well, sweetie, it's time to go."

Sam couldn't take his eyes off Bella.

In fact, hadn't been able to look away since he first saw her when he'd picked her up and still couldn't now that the limo was pulling up outside the theater. Her grandmother's 1940s Bentley, just ahead of them, inched to a stop by the red-carpet walkway.

Not that he'd been able to talk to Bella or, more important, touch her since her brother Max and his fiancée Dana rode with them, relegating everything to small talk. Of course their presence also helped him stay the course in keeping enough distance from her so Bella would come to him on her own.

The limo inched toward the red carpet spread from the edge of the curb all the way into the sprawling steps leading into the historic theater. He kept his arm along the back of the seat only allowing his fingers to lightly brush her neck, about all the temptation his libido could stand. Bella presented a mix of pristine untouchable beauty in that ivory creation, yet the strapless top of the dress tempted him with the creamy curves of her shoulders and generous breasts.

He could envision her wearing that diamond necklace and nothing else.

Patience.

Camera flashes clicked at strobelike speed outside

the limo's tinted windows. Security guards had the street blocked to outside traffic, cordoning off the area for the slow parade of vehicles toward the theater. People dressed to see and be seen strode up the red carpet, posing for photos, stopping for the occasional impromptu interview with entertainment reporters.

Fans packed either side behind the gold ropes lining the path. Bodyguards in tuxedos did more to keep the fans in check than any decorative cord.

Just ahead, the Bentley's chauffeur opened a door. Family matriarch Lillian Hudson stepped from the limousine, aided by both her sons. Markus and David wore traditional tuxedos and composed faces. No one would guess they were at each other's throats because David's long ago affair with Markus's wife Sabrina had been explosively revealed.

The brothers were putting on a good show at civility for their mother. This was almost certainly her last Hudson Studios movie premiere.

Lillian Hudson walked up the red carpet, her steps even if slow, a son remaining on either side. Sam could see subtle signs they were supporting her. But from what little he'd heard about the woman, he was certain she wouldn't even consider using a walker or wheelchair at this particular event.

A strong lady, no question. With her auburn hair, Sam could see flashes of Bella in this woman. However, apparently even Lillian's strength couldn't beat the breast cancer.

Was the hair a wig due to her treatments? If so, it

was a damn good one. She hid her illness well. Somehow, she made the sedate pace seem regal rather than frail in her deep blue gown and sapphires.

A true timeless beauty and star.

Bella's head was turned toward the window, her eyes sparkling, as were her future sister-in-law's. Even her brother seated across from them cleared his throat.

Sam squeezed Bella's shoulder. "Come on. No crying. You beautiful ladies will wreck your makeup."

Bella pulled a wobbly smile, leaning into his touch. "You're right. It's just emotional seeing her tonight."

She needed him. A surge of protectiveness shot through him.

He started to answer her but the opening door cut him short. "Your fans await."

She held his gaze for a second, confusion whispering through her eyes. Her hand fell to his thigh. "Thank you."

Without another word, she turned away, stepped out and waved. His leg damn near on fire from her simple quick caress, Sam followed, palming the small of her back. The flashbulbs clicked as fast as ticker tape, blinding him. As much as he enjoyed touching Bella, he hated dog-and-pony shows, but he would put on a good face for her. She deserved her moment.

Then the reporters' questions started in a flurry of shouts.

"Miss Hudson, tell us more about this new man with you."

"How did you meet?"

"What happened to Ridley Sinclair?"

"Did you break Ridley's heart?"

A host from a major network talk show—someone who could stand on the red carpet side of those golden ropes—rushed forward with her microphone. Bella squeezed Sam's arm in a signal to stop.

The reporter screeched to a halt, her plastic surgery all too evident up close, with eyebrows millimeters away from her hairline. "Look who we have here, the leading actress of *Honor*, Bella Hudson. Good evening, Bella. You look marvelous darling. Tell us about your dress and jewelry."

Bella posed for the camera, showing off a side angle of her gown while a camera swooped an extra spotlight on her. "I'm wearing a Marchesa original." Her hand swept up to her neck and her ears. "But the diamonds are totally Hudson, gifts from my lovely grandmother who this film honors tonight."

The reporter leaned closer, winking at her camera lens before turning to Bella. "Our viewers are dying to know if it's true that you and Ridley Sinclair are no longer an item."

Bella tucked nearer to his side. "Sam Garrison is an important part of my life."

"Garrison? Oh! One of American's most eligible billionaire bachelors." The reporter's eyebrows disappeared into her brunette coif. "Who called it quits between you and your leading man in *Honor*?"

Sam angled toward the mic. "I have to confess to

CATHERINE MANN   107

being the bad guy here. My apologies to Mr. Sinclair, but once I saw Bella, I knew I had to have her."

Bella smiled up at him in gratitude that the reporter must have mistaken for adoration since she sighed and dramatically fanned her face. "Oh, my, the steam factor is hot here tonight, ladies and gentlemen."

Sam cupped Bella's shoulder. "We should move on. We wouldn't want to hold up the show."

He ushered her through two more interviews, and couldn't help but admire her ease with the whole chaotic mess. He wanted to get his show on the road and park themselves in the theater.

A group of females screamed to his left. He jolted, ready to body block any threat from out of control fans…. Only to see the female attention was directed firmly behind them.

Ridley—the rat and moron who'd let Bella slip away—stepped out of the limousine with a *Sports Illustrated* swimsuit model on his arm. A moody lock of hair stayed perfectly styled over one eye.

Bella stiffened, her smile brittle.

Sam brushed his mouth over her ear. "I hear that anorexic airhead's vanity dog has a boring smile."

Bella relaxed against him, tipped her head back and laughed. The reporters turned their frenzy back onto her. Cameras clicked away, the flashes firmly on the two of them while Ridley helped his date untangle her heel from the hem of her skimpy Band-Aid dress.

The sound of Bella's happiness beat the hell out of all the bells he'd ever heard from the French churches. She sang through his veins more and more. Patience was paying off, but he wasn't done playing his hand. Time to make his big move toward getting the press talking and winning Bella's favor.

He escorted her past the last of the outdoor media into the crush of servers and early arrivers inside the lobby, decorated evergreen trees towering up into the cathedral ceiling. Twinkling lights and gilded angels graced the fragrant boughs. Red roses and poinsettias filled massive urns. Garland looped the gold rails leading into the historic theater.

And a fresh batch of reporters waited. Sam might hate the profession on principle, but he wasn't against using them to his advantage for Bella.

He paused at the top of the lengthy staircase, skimmed the corner of her mouth. "Merry Christmas, Bella."

He slid a black-velvet jewelry box into her hand, the sort that contained bracelets. A photographer elbowed a supporting actor out of the way to thrust her telephoto lens closer. Little did any of them know what was *really* inside.

Sam ducked his head closer to hers again. "You may not want the press to see what's actually in here."

Her eyes went wide, her pupils dilating with excitement. Tucking the box close to her chest, Bella untied the bow, creaked open the box and found...

He'd given her a small designer dog collar. Pink. With an engraved tag that read Muffin.

Smiling, she tipped her face up to thank him and

Sam sealed his mouth to hers. Nothing long or drawn out, but unmistakably romantic for the cameras.

Enough to make the press spread the news—and knock him on his ass.

Bella blinked up at him wide-eyed, a little confused. The single kiss had rocked him more than he'd expected. His hands-off policy the past few days had messed with his restraint. He'd scripted the kiss but sure as hell hadn't planned on how much it would floor him.

Sam slid his hand to the small of her back, gently urging her back into the moment. "Let's go see a movie."

He'd come here for her. Now he had to figure out how to stay around after the premiere so he could see what surprises their next kiss might have in store.

Eight

Bella settled into her seat in the historic theater, balconies overhead packed in the sellout premiere. She should be taking note of everything around her, cementing this breakout moment in her memory. Yet she could only think of Sam beside her, his thoughtful gift in her beaded ivory handbag.

His kiss still lingered on her lips.

While Sam asserted that looks didn't matter, his strong presence certainly appealed to her on an elemental level—tall and striking in his traditional tuxedo and clean-shaven face. Surprisingly, he'd been patient with the reporters even though she knew that sort of media fanfare must be driving him nuts. Yet, he'd put up with it smoothly for her.

The biggest surprise of all, though? Seeing Ridley. She'd been so nervous about crossing paths with him, of the stab of pain and betrayal she expected his presence to bring and...*nothing*. Ridley actually looked small and rather foolish in his bolo tie up next to Sam who didn't need props to carry a room with his charisma.

She leaned toward Sam and whispered, "Thank you for my lovely gift."

"You're welcome." His aftershave teased her senses. "Merry Christmas."

"I have something for you, too." The day they'd gone shopping in Paris she'd bought him a little brass antique bell to remember her by.

"Is it what I really want?" he asked, his intent clear from the wicked glint in his eyes.

Her breasts tightened with awareness, anticipation. *Undiluted want.* "I don't believe what you're referring to would fit under a tree."

"I work out. I'm very limber."

She laughed, drawing eyes toward them. She lowered her voice again so it wouldn't be heard over the WWII tunes piped in from the sound system. "Why didn't you wait for me after the *Tonight Show* interview?"

She'd been dying to ask him ever since they'd met at her place to rendezvous with the limo, but Dana and Max had been there, prohibiting her from delving into any conversation about David.

"I ran into a business acquaintance and we had to

leave." He tugged a lone lock of hair along the back of her neck. "You look incredible tonight."

"Don't try and sidetrack me." She knew full well how easily he could distract her mindless through just a touch. "I know you ran into David. Why did you make him leave?"

He stroked the back of her neck, along her vertebra sending delicious shivers down her spine. "I hope you're not going to bite my head off here like you did over the Charlotte incident. It won't go well with the image we're working to portray."

Trust was tough, but she couldn't miss how he'd had her feelings in mind, how he'd cared enough to try and shield her. "Actually, I want to say thank you. I really would rather not talk to him at all anytime soon." *If ever.*

"You're welcome."

His somber gray gaze held her still. He simply stared at her as if no one else in this overflowing theater existed. Memories of his sensually intuitive touch in France flooded her senses, tempting her to throw caution out the window and dive headfirst into an affair with Sam. The heat of his gaze shut out the rest of the world, her attention dipping to his mouth as she wondered how his kiss would taste.

Why not indulge? At the moment, she couldn't seem to come up with a single argument against giving in to the demands of her desire.

The lights dimmed, forcing her to divert her attention forward to the movie screen. She'd seen the rough cut of the film and of course knew every scene by heart. Still there was something magical about watching a movie—one including her—play out officially.

Sam's hand slid over hers. For appearances or support? She linked her fingers with his, the rough texture of his callused grip sending a fresh wash of tingles over her.

Sam's thumb stroking the sensitive inside of her wrist, Bella watched her grandparents' love story unfold, starting with how her grandfather had worked in Marseille. A U.S. soldier, he'd been part of a spy cell for the Allied Forces. The screen scanned a panoramic view of the small sea port—the very one near Sam's hotel. In fact she'd enjoyed that view during supper the night they'd made love.

The present and past merged in her mind as a young Charles Hudson met and was captivated by Lillian Colbert, a spirited young cabaret singer in a nightclub. Their romance traveled a rocky path as Charles suspected the sad-eyed beauty could be a collaborator with the occupying German army.

Bella gripped Sam's hand, the turmoil of her grandmother's life surging through her much as the musical score swelled throughout the theater. Bella had said those words that Lillian had lived, linking them even beyond the appearance and blood they shared.

She could feel the agony of her grandmother's grief when Charles was injured and on the run. Lillian rescued him and hid him, first in her tiny apartment above the club, then forced to take refuge at a friend's country estate. Bella's heart pounded with exhaustion, fear, exhilaration as she relived the chase scene when Lillian and Charles made their getaway.

Her fingers went numb and she realized she'd been squeezing Sam's hand so hard she'd cut off circulation. She pressed her palm to her fluttering stomach, even knowing what came next, cheering inside when Charles discovered that Lillian was actually working for the French Resistance. The risks and bravery of her grandparents blew Bella away all over again. Under constant threat of discovery, Charles and Lillian teamed up to further the Resistance's cause, secretly marrying.

The scene blended to their wedding night—passionate, explosive and apparently a part of the movie Sam was not enjoying. His jaw visibly clenched as Ridley/Charles kissed down her neck, tugging the simple string at the top of her peasant blouse. The scene wasn't overly graphic, shot mostly in close-ups of their faces or a far away silhouette with their bodies under the covers. The window behind them gusted loose curtains around them, the wind increasing with the rise of their passion, ending with close-ups of their hands clenched together over her head, tighter, then slowly unfurling.

Had Sam actually growled?

She couldn't deny a hint of excitement even as she wanted to roll her eyes. She leaned toward him, her mouth to his ear. "I wore a body stocking under the covers for that scene."

"I didn't ask," he said tight and low.

"I wanted you to know."

He grunted.

"Ridley wore tighty whities."

A smile ticked the corner of Sam's mouth before she settled back into her seat and returned her attention to the movie alive with the liberation of France.

Charles had to leave his new bride behind and return to the fight in Germany, but during their tearful farewell he promised to return at the end of the war. Battle weary, he kept his promise and reclaimed his waiting wife. Bella watched the camera pull out on a panorama of her grandparents passionately kissing, profiled against the Marseille shore.

And to Bella, those two people on the screen *were* her grandparents.

The audience exploded with applause and cheers, a standing ovation rippling to life. As words scrolled across detailing Charles and Lillian's life together in the United States, Bella's mind swirled with memories of sitting on her grandfather's knee while he humbly told the stories behind his many medals. She missed him, could almost smell his cigar smoke. They all could have used his calm logic right now to set their family back on track.

Although she knew she couldn't possibly miss him nearly as much as her grandmother did. Their love had been special. Rare.

With the triumph of a beautiful romance surging inside her heart, would Bella now know when it came to her life? She couldn't settle for an affair. She was an all-or-nothing person.

Sam downed his club soda during the after party bash hosted at the Hudson family estate on Loma Vista Drive in Beverly Hills. It was mind boggling how many people chose to spend their Christmas night at the Hudson home, but then Hollywood was all about being seen in the right places.

He'd had enough of their schmoozing for an entire decade.

In particular he'd had enough of watching slimy wheeler-dealers in the industry put their paws all over Bella. Not that she seemed to do anything to stop them. She smiled and flirted and damn near drove him over the brink as live band music grated in his ears.

Uniformed waiters wove through the crowded living room with canapés and champagne. Having overseen the decor for five Garrison hotels, he studied Bella's childhood mansion as he stood in the formal living room. The interior was very French Provincial, but not overtly stuffy, with antiques he would wage money had come from around the world. Marble floors stretched throughout a grand foyer with a mammoth evergreen nestled between double-wide staircases, pastel lights glittering along the branches. Hand painted wallpapers and fifteen-foot ceilings all made for a classically grand mansion.

"Sit down."

His head whipped around to find Lillian Hudson tucked in a wingback chair by the garland-strewn fireplace. "Pardon?"

She rested a thin hand on his arm, her veins showing through near translucent skin. "Sit down, young man, before you start a brawl."

Sam eased into the wingback beside her, releasing the button on his tuxedo jacket. "My mother raised me better than that, ma'am."

"I'm glad to hear it, but even my Charles lost some of his silver-spoon ways after seeing one of my smoky on-screen kisses." She waved her hand, only a slight shake betraying her health crisis. "All of this is just for show. Bella's a good girl."

He really didn't want to talk about Bella's sex life with her grandmother. "Yes, ma'am. I understand that."

His eyes lingered on Bella still in her off-white dress from the premiere. Men pressed drinks into her hand that he noticed she stashed on the mantel behind her.

Seeing her on the big screen had impressed the hell out of him. He'd heard of her growing reputation in indy films so he'd expected a decent performance. He hadn't been prepared for her to blow him away. He admired her talent, although he would be hard-pressed to get that love scene out of his head.

Without question, *Honor* would catapult her to the next level in her career.

"She's having a difficult time right now." Lillian leaned on the arm of the chair, angling closer, her blue eyes still bright and alert. "Her mother and father are just pretending to be polite tonight for my sake, but I know they're still separated."

"She has told me about what happened with her parents." He gently skirted the issue of the affair that produced Bella.

"Really? That's surprising." Her gaze darted to her wayward younger son David who smartly kept a full room's distance between himself and the rest of his family. "I'm ashamed of what David did. I'm afraid I spoiled him with my pampering. I should have treated him as I did my oldest."

The insight was interesting, but he'd watched his mother blame herself for another man's actions for too long to let Lillian go to her grave with that weighing on her heart. "Ma'am, if you'll pardon me for a moment, I believe adults are responsible for their own actions. No blaming others for their own mistakes."

A slow smile spread over her face with a charming allure that broadcast well what a heartbreaker she must have been in her day. "I like you, young man."

He patted her hand gently. "The feeling is mutual, ma'am."

A light scowl puckered her forehead. "Be good to Bella or I will haunt you from the grave."

Crap. What did a guy say to something like that? He wasn't used to being caught off guard. In fact, never was. "Umm, ma'am—"

"Loosen up, young man." She patted his face. "I'm making a joke." Her hand fell away limply, her spark giving way to exhaustion in a flash. She reached to her other side to an older woman in a simple black dress. "Hannah? I am ready to retire."

Sam helped Lillian to her feet and offered his arm until she was safely away from the jostling crowd.

He pivoted back around, searching the crush for Bella. All he had to do was look for the largest pack of men, since they seemed drawn to her like magnets to metal. He retrieved his drink and watched, reminding himself that he would be the one finishing out the night with her.

And he intended to make damn sure her dreams included *him*.

Her hand tucked in the crook of Sam's arm, Bella strolled leisurely across the Hudson Manor lawn toward her home in the guesthouse. Her filmy gold wrap trailed behind her in the gentle evening breeze on a standard sixty-degree December evening. Champagne and success left her slightly tipsy, even if she had fed plenty of bubbly to unsuspecting potted ferns.

A looming angel fountain spewed water backlit with Christmas red. White lights swayed along branches of trees lining her path past the tennis courts back to her place.

She couldn't have dreamed up a more perfect setting—or a more intriguing man.

Bella tipped her face up to Sam, her heels sinking in the soft earth. "Thank you for sharing your Christmas with me."

"I'm here to serve."

She looked away, staring at the ground to keep from tripping over roots. "I appreciate how you handled the publicity about Ridley. Even my family bought our act." She glanced up again. "Maybe you should be nominated for an Academy Award."

He palmed her back, steering her around a wrought-iron bench. "I'm not acting when I say how much I want you."

"I thought we agreed no sex talk." Her beaded bag dangled from her arm, her gift for Sam inside.

"No—" he smiled "—you said there wouldn't be sex. You never specified anything about talk of sex."

She didn't want to wade into those waters, not tonight when surely it would lead them into an argument—or lure her into a temptation she wasn't sure she could resist. Hadn't she realized tonight that she couldn't tread into this awkward terrain with him? In spite of her behavior earlier this week, she wasn't a fling sort of girl.

Bella sprinted forward and turned to face him, walking backward. "Tell me about your family."

"That was a fairly transparent attempt to change the subject." He stayed step to step with her in a near dance move.

"As long as you get the message." She tugged his bow tie. "Isn't your family missing you over the holidays?"

"I'm an adult. As for immediate family, there's only my mother. She never had another child, so I don't have any siblings, just lots of cousins. Mom ventures out of her island hideaway to spend most holidays with them in South Beach. They all have kids and she enjoys being with children at Christmas."

"She must be expecting some grandchildren from you." Had she really blurted that? She stumbled to a stop at the base of the three steps leading up to her cottage.

"That's none of my business. Forget I said it." Flustered at her blunder, she rested her hands on his chest without thinking. "Thank you again for coming with me tonight."

His eyes went from guarded to predatory in a spine-tingling flash as sure as the stars overhead.

"My pleasure." He leaned toward her, his mouth hovering just over hers, the heat of his breath teasing her with a phantom touch. "If I had my way, I would pleasure you even more tonight. If we *were* still having sex, I would take you back to the limousine. I would tell the chauffeur to drive until I say otherwise. Then I would close the privacy window."

Her very vivid artistic imagination flourished to life with possibilities for playing out a sexy fantasy she'd never tried before. She started to tell him to stop, but what harm could come from words?

"All night long I've been thinking about taking your hair down." He tugged the lone loose curl, his knuckles grazing between her shoulder blades. "Of how it would feel tumbling down into my hands."

She struggled to keep her eyes from fluttering

closed. "All the hairspray could wreak havoc on your allergies."

He laughed low. "I'm willing to risk it." His hands skimmed her arms to cup her waist. "The zipper along your back has driven me crazy all evening long. If I tugged it down, would you be wearing a bra or are you totally bare for me?"

Her breath hitched somewhere around her ribcage. She should make up a tale of boring underwear and save herself the extra ache when she sent him away tonight. But the truth fell out on a breathless, "The bra is built into the dress."

He growled. "Since we're not having sex, I have to guess you are only wearing panties."

She nodded weakly. "Tap pants, actually."

"Satin?"

She nodded again.

"Creamy colored like the dress. Like your skin. I still remember the silky feel of it under my mouth, sheened with champagne. I couldn't even drink the stuff tonight for fear it would send me out of control from wanting you." His lips grazed hers, just barely, but more than enough to ignite her flames through her veins. "God, you look amazing. Every man in the room was thinking what a lucky guy I am."

His words swirled through her already champagne-woozy mind and lowered defenses. She clenched his lapels, stretching up, craving a full-out kiss.

He slid away at the very last second, his hot breath caressing her neck. "If we were having sex, I would skim away your tap pants so we could celebrate in the best way. Don't you agree?"

She swayed toward him, entranced. Aching. He kept his mouth poised just below her ear, so near her eyes drifted closed as her body already anticipated a nip along her earlobe, warm kisses down the sensitive curve of her neck down to her shoulder. Her head fell back limply at merely the possibility.

Damn it.

She straightened upright again. What was she doing? Only a few hours ago she'd sat in the theater determined to follow an all-or-nothing approach to any future relationships. Yet here she already stood wanting more than anything to say to hell with it all and spend the night naked with Sam, celebrating the premiere the old-fashioned way.

He tapped her lips. "No need to answer. Because according to you we're not sleeping together, something that won't change unless you tell me otherwise."

She wanted to say yes, her body positively on fire for his touch, but the hope from the end of *Honor* still prodded her to want more, reminding her that trust and forever were rare gifts in a world full of lies and broken relationships.

She couldn't miss the competitive gleam in his eyes, an emotion that would muddy the waters of any possible relationship because she wouldn't be sure of his motives.

Did he want her?

Or merely want to win?

Her indecision must have shown because he eased away, scrubbing a hand over his jaw. "All right then." Sam backed down the steps. "Merry Christmas, Bella."

He pivoted back toward the line of limos along the driveway. She gripped the railing to keep from bolting after him. Her purse thudded to the porch, jingling a reminder that she had forgotten to give him the Christmas bell.

As she watched Sam climb into the limousine, she wasn't sure if she'd just made a stand—or thrown away a once-in-a-lifetime chance.

Nine

Four weeks later, Bella flopped backward on her wrought-iron bed, the train on her burgundy Vera Wang gown swooshing around her. She should be turning cartwheels tonight after winning the Screen Actors Guild's Best Actress Award. *Honor* also picked up Best Picture and Best Director, a real coup for a breakout surprise hit.

Accepting that trophy had been amazing, and the after party advantageous as she schmoozed with Hollywood bigwigs until the wee hours with Sam standing by her. During the party—in fact over the past month—he had been the perfect escort and a total gentleman, honoring her request for no sex.

Damn.

That man was driving her absolutely batty.

Bella rolled to her side, staring out the window as the first morning rays shot golden streaks across the sky. Besides escorting her to both the Golden Globe and Screen Actors Guild Awards, he'd taken her out to elaborate dinners and society functions to feed publicity as *Honor* continued to dominate the theaters and the news.

He'd also surprised her with a lighthearted day of fun at Disneyland, followed by a stop at a local animal shelter to drop off a monster-big donation check. Most touching, he'd patiently joined her for quiet dinners with Lillian in her grandmother's chambers as the end stages of her cancer confined her.

Afterward, Sam would walk her across the lawn and drop her off at her door with a peck on top of her head like she was a flipping kid. Just as he'd done again tonight.

She dropped a pillow over her face to muffle her shout of frustration.

Yet how could she complain? He'd followed her request for helping dispel any rumors she might be carrying a torch for Ridley.

After Sam had escorted her to the Golden Globe Awards earlier in the month, magazines and television media had reported everything from supposed matching love tattoos to a secret wedding in Las Vegas. Gossip rags even digitally altered an image of her with a small baby bump that circulated the news prominently enough for Dana to rush across the lawn and demand Bella hike up her shirt to prove she wasn't expecting.

She pitched aside the pillow and scooped up Muffin from the foot of the bed. "What should I do about this guy?"

Muffin cocked her head to the side, her snaggle-tooth look bringing reminders of Sam's teasing label of a Billy Idol snarl. Bella ruffled a hand along her dog's bristly fur. "I guess you're not able to help out too much on this one, huh?"

If ever she'd needed someone to talk to, someone she could trust not to spill her secrets… She straightened. That very person was just across the lawn. Her grandmother. Lillian had always been an early riser and was now even more so since she slept in short spurts throughout the day and night.

Bella rolled from her bed to her feet, rushed to her closet and yanked out the first thing her hands fell on. She slid the side zipper down on the form-hugging gown, kicking the train out of the way and peeling the dress down. She shimmied into jeans, tugged a V-necked tight T-shirt over her strapless bra and left the rubies on. Hopping into her heels on the way out the door, she snagged the trophy she'd won and called for Muffin to follow her.

Breathlessly, she raced across the lawn, her loose French twist shaking free with each reckless wobbly step as she sprinted past the angel fountain. Muffin trotted closely at her heels, up the steps and into the foyer. The little dog dashed toward the kitchen where the cook always kept special puppy treats.

Bella's heels clicked over the marble floor on her way to Grandmere's first-floor quarters. A live-in nurse had moved into the bedroom next door to be close after Lillian had been released from the hospital.

Gathering her tattered composure, Bella tapped lightly on the door.

The door creaked open an inch, the housekeeper Hannah on the other side. "Oh, Ms. Bella, come on in. Mrs. Hudson is awake and she always perks up when she sees you."

"Thank you, Hannah." Bella squeezed her arm and stepped inside. "Good morning, Grandmere. I brought you something."

She placed her Screen Actors Guild Best Actress Award on the bedside table. Already, she breathed easier now that the familiar air of the soothing room surrounded her. Tall vases of flowers—live and silk—filled the airy room along with Lillian's personal photo collection. She'd met dignitaries from around the world in her career, starting with her work in the French cabarets to the years she spent as the toast of Tinseltown.

There were also pictures of her with other stars, but there were many, many more of her surrounded by her family. Bella appeared in a handful of the images framed in matching ivory mats with gilt frames, the spill of Hudsons around her. And on Lillian's beside table rested her most treasured photo of all, one taken the day she and her husband eloped. So much love emanated from Lillian's family gallery.

Not until recently had Bella started to look for hints of unhappiness in the scenes from her childhood.

Her grandmother moved her arm from over her eyes, the pinch of pain at the corners of her mouth easing into a smile. "Thank you, sweet Bella. You've all made me so happy with the movie. First Golden Globe Awards and now this. Come tell me about tonight's ceremony."

Wearing a deeply pleated linen nightgown with a matching wrapper, Lillian still clothed herself with the simple grace that had marked her unpretentious style all her life. A blue ribbon held a cameo locket about her neck, the keepsake memento Bella had played with as a child. She knew if she pressed the tiny latch on one side, she would find a black-and-white picture of her grandfather in uniform beside the image of a tiny cottage along a winding French river.

"That's why I'm here." She winged a prayer for forgiveness for that little lie.

The housekeeper gathered up a breakfast tray with most of the food untouched.

The nurse checked the IV drip, before backing toward the door. "I'm going to step out for a few minutes and let you two have some privacy. Just ring if you need anything," she said before following Hannah out the door.

Her grandmother weakly adjusted the pillows piled behind her, her head swathed in a rose satin scarf rather than her wig. She'd resisted having a hospital bed brought into her room, insisting she would spend her final days in the bed she'd shared with her beloved husband.

"Sit here, Bella dear." Lillian patted the spot beside her.

The hint of a French lilt in her voice washed over Bella with warm familiarity. She had spent so many hours as a child, curled in her grandmother's lap listening to stories and singing together.

"I'm not so little anymore." She settled carefully onto the edge, her heart squeezing with pain over how fast time flew, how soon her grandmother would be gone. She fought back tears Lillian had long ago told her she didn't want to see.

"Come closer and quit worrying you will break me. I have wonderful painkillers." She waggled her arm with an IV taped in place. "Remember when you used to run in here early in the morning so we could talk before the rest of the house came to life?"

Beautiful memories flooded her with a joy and peace she desperately needed right now. "Grandpere always went to work early and I knew I could have you to myself." Bella swung her legs up, crossing them to sit by her grandmother, the underlying antiseptic air of a sick room mingling with Lillian's scent, an old Chanel formula she had worn her entire life. "I wish you could have gone with us to the awards ceremony last night."

"Hannah and I watched every moment on my television." A plasma-screen television had been mounted over the fireplace mantel once Lillian became bed-bound. "The awards are nice, but beyond that, I am so proud of you and pleased with how you portrayed me in the movie. You did yourself and the family very proud."

Lillian's compliment meant…everything. Stifling a blush, Bella traced the intricate pattern on the gold brocade spread. "All I did was bring your wonderful spirit to the screen. You're amazing, Grandmere."

As much as she had longed for the lead actress role in *Honor*, she'd also been terrified of falling short. Her grandmother was a remarkable woman with an unmistakably dynamic presence, a presence that had made her a big screen star in her own right.

A twinkle lit Lillian's blue eyes. "Your young man looked quite handsome, too, although a mite irritated about those men fawning over you." She peered above her bifocals with a wicked rather than censuring twinkle. "That dress of yours was rather risqué, don't you think?"

Sam had actually noticed the men speaking to her? Could have fooled her. "I've looked at your photo albums, Grandmere," Bella teased, "and you've worn a risqué dress or two yourself."

Lillian laughed lightly. "That I have, that I have." Her laughter faded. "I'm glad nothing came of your relationship with that Ridley."

"I thought it would make you nostalgic to see the two of us together since we made the movie, revived those days when you fell in love. He even looks like Grandpere." Had that perhaps been a reason she let herself be drawn in by Ridley's playboy charm? In some hope of living out her grandmother's grand romance for real? A disquieting thought, to say the least.

"He may have looked like your grandfather and he may be a fine actor on screen, but off screen? *Non, non.* The man was nothing like my Charles. Besides, it rarely works for two actors to marry each other. You've chosen well with your new man. He has his own power and success in a different arena from yours."

"I'm glad you approve." Bella looked away quickly, afraid her grandmother would read the truth in her eyes. Whatever the truth was right now.

"Tell me more about him. He is so quietly polite during the dinners we've had. He always leaves you and me to do the gabbing." Fresh air toyed with the curtains at the window.

"Well, in spite of what the media reports, I am definitely not pregnant." Bella hitched her shirt up to just below her breasts.

Grandmere clapped a hand over her mouth and laughed, a raspy sound but unmistakable mirth. Too soon, the laughs turned to coughs.

Bella passed her grandmother a cup of ice water with a bent straw. Lillian sipped with labored draws until her throat cleared again.

"Thank you, dear. Of course I know you are not expecting. We have always talked about everything.

That is why I am surprised I haven't heard more from you about Sam."

It wasn't for lack of having him in her thoughts that Bella hadn't shared more. She was so confused about how she felt, about what was happening between them, she didn't know what to think, let alone what to say. "We're still in the early stage, waiting to see what happens."

Lillian's mouth pursed thoughtfully. "Trust is difficult. The Garrisons have had their problems like any family, but they persevere. I respect that. Your grandfather always said they were ruthless but honest in the business world. You'll need someone that strong to keep you grounded in this profession. I found that kind of man in your grandfather."

Grandmere thought Sam was like Grandpere? Now that had never crossed her mind and she wasn't quite sure what to do with the notion yet.

"Bella?" Lillian pulled her back into the moment. "I know you've suffered some hurtful surprises of late, but be kind to your father."

Startled, Bella wanted to cry out *which one*? Markus, the man who made her his pampered princess for twenty-five years? Or David, the man who'd wrecked her parents' marriage with the affair, the man who'd been nothing more than sperm donor in making her?

She held her tongue, however. Lillian was entitled to blurt random dictates like this since—with a heart-lurching ache—Bella knew grandmother wouldn't be around much longer to direct the stage around her the way she'd done with a firm but gracious hand her whole life.

Except Grandmere had a reputation for petting David, her one flaw. Had David been a bad seed, which led Grandmere to favor him because she knew he was weaker than his brother? Or had she made him weak spoiling him?

They would never know for sure, however one thing was certain. David Hudson led a self-centered life, wreaking havoc all around him.

She couldn't burden her grandmother with her own heartache, not now. The comfort of Lillian's presence would have to be enough. "Of course, I'll be nice to him, Grandmere."

"Good, good. I knew you would do the right thing. You've always been the tender-hearted one. You may have inherited my temper, but you never could hold a grudge." Her grandmother sighed, sagging back into her satin-covered pillows. "I am tired. Please get Hannah to come sit with me while I take a nap."

Bella squelched the twinge of disappointment that she hadn't really broached the topic she most needed to discuss. Guilt seared her throat that she'd spent precious moments dancing around the matters that were most important to her.

Bella pressed the call button and within seconds the housekeeper rushed through the door. Stout but spry, with graying hair and kind hazel-green eyes, Hannah had been with the family for thirty years, always making sure the large and boisterous family ran smoothly. "I'm here, ma'am. You just rest."

Bella eyed her grandmother, panic welling. How many "naps" did Lillian have left? The doctors had said it could be any day now. They'd been hopeful for more time, however, since Lillian had already outlived medical expectations. "I'll stay. I don't mind, really. I want to."

"No, no, you go," Lillian insisted. "I need to take my medicines and change into a fresh gown first. Please, it will make me happy to think of you with your Sam."

She looked deeper into her grandmother's weary eyes and saw beyond the words to her need for privacy with her pain. Bella leaned to hug her gently, carefully avoiding the IV. "I love you, Grandmere."

"I love you, too." She cupped Bella's face. "Be happy."

Bella slid from the bed, backing toward the door so she could smile at her grandmother until the very…last…second.

Once in the hall, she sagged back against the wall and let the tears flow. Heartache and helplessness flooded through her, pushing more tears streaming down her face, more than she thought one person could shed. This hurt far more than she'd felt that night in Marseille when she'd ended up in Sam's bed for a few hours of forgetfulness.

Grief threatened to drive her to her knees. There was so little time left. Thinking about how quickly life could change forever made her revaluate her all or nothing mindset when it came to Sam. Life was fleeting. Right now was what truly mattered, this moment, because there might not be another.

She stiffened her spine, straightening away from the wall and swiping the back of her wrist over her eyes. She was a fighter like her grandmother. What she wanted, she went after.

And right now, she wanted Sam.

Sam sat behind the desk in his executive office at the new L.A. Garrison Grande Hotel due to open within another two months. Construction noise echoed a floor above as workers reinstalled crown molding. He should go up there and inspect the progress, stretch his legs, air his mind out about the headache item that headlined today's gossip columns. He pitched aside two newspapers folded open to the offending item—a thorn from his past coming back to jab him on a day he was running on fumes from the late night with Bella at the awards ceremony and party.

Although in retrospect, he should have seen this coming. He creaked back in the oversize leather chair, the only addition he'd made to the sparse temporary office space. A permanent manager would be hired once the place opened. That had been his plan from the beginning since this wasn't his type of town with its see-and-be-seen attitude.

He should be used to this kind of crap in the newspaper by now. At least Bella appeared immune to all the gossip, in fact seeming to welcome anything that advanced her acting career. So much so, there were times at those functions where it was all he could do not to deck the latest industry letch looking down her dress.

His phone buzzed just as his doorknob turned. The intercom echoed with his interim secretary's high pitched voice, "Mr. Garrison, you have a—"

Visitor.

Bella stood framed in the doorway, her hair a damn sexy mess. She struck a wide legged pose in red heels, jeans and a curve hugging T-shirt with a ruby and diamond necklace that cost more than most cars. Given her wild-eyed look, he assumed she must have seen the latest bombshell in the newspapers.

His secretary, a pencil jammed in her hair bun, peeked over Bella's shoulder. "Uh, Mr. Garrison…"

"It's okay. Close the door and hold my calls, please." Once the lock clicked, he gathered his words to explain. "Bella, about—"

She held up a finger, tossing her head, flicking her fiery hair over her shoulder. "Don't say anything. Me first, because I don't want to waste even a single second here."

Ohhh-kay. That would give him more time to gauge her mood.

She flung aside her oversize gold purse.

Thud.

She peeled her T-shirt up and off.

Whoosh.

What the hell? He damn near choked on his tongue. Bella sent the wisp of cotton sailing in a fluttery white flight across the room to land on his computer.

Apparently she wasn't here about the latest in the news. He'd been biding his time when it came to her no-sex request, waiting—painfully at times—for her to come to him. He just hadn't expected her turn around to be quite so dramatic.

One hip jutting, she stood across from him in a red strapless bra and the glittering ruby necklace, her low-rise jeans displaying her diamond belly-button ring and a mouth-drying expanse of creamy skin. "So Sam Garrison, has anyone ever told you you're a tease?"

He scrubbed a hand over his jaw to keep his shock from showing. "Run that by me again?"

She strutted forward, her wild hair and curves and do-me heels spiking his heart rate through the roof. She slid a hand into her pocket, pulled it back out and slapped it on his desk, leaving behind...

A condom packet.

"Okay, big guy, it's time to put up or shut up."

Ten

Bella bolstered her nerve, determined to see this through with Sam, to live in the moment. She'd certainly succeeded in shocking him silent.

She planted her heels deeper in the lush carpet, the rest of the office, however, was sparse. He'd obviously set this up as a temporary operating post with a large mahogany desk, a media center in the corner and one long leather couch—presumably for naps.

A lone banker's lamp rested on the corner of his desk beside newspapers. He'd replaced the on/off chain with the small bell she'd finally given him one evening after supper with Lillian.

His sentimental gesture filled her with reassurance

she was doing the right thing by coming here. By seducing *him*.

His steely eyes narrowed sensually. "I take that to mean the no-sex rule is now null and void."

"You would be right." She tapped him on the chest right over his red silk tie, nudging him backward until he reached his large, leather office chair. Empowerment surged through her. There was something to be said for living in the moment. "But I'm the one in charge today."

With a gentle two-handed shove on his shoulders, she urged him to sit. He could have stopped this at any time. No question who held the physical strength edge here. Yet for some reason he seemed to be through with his tease-and-tempt games.

Was it really as simple as he'd been waiting for her to make the first move all this time? Her pulse quickened at the thought he truly wanted her that much. That perhaps going out together wasn't just about scaring off matchmaking mamas in search of a wealthy son-in-law.

Sam had a lot more going for him than his bank balance. Not the least of which was the searing look he gave her that made her knees weak and her breath catch. Pulse fluttering wildly, Bella toyed with the clasp between her breasts and freed her bra. Cool air whispered over her, her nipples tightening in response, tingling in oversensitive need for a firmer caress.

He whistled low and long. "Woman, you are driving—"

"Shh." She leaned forward, pressing a finger to his lips and bringing her breasts closer to him. Sam's tangy aftershave mixed with the scent of freshly painted walls.

His hands crept up and she clamped his wrists, denying herself for the moment. But for a moment only.

"This is my show, Sam Garrison. Unless you have an objection."

He shook his head slowly, his gaze locked steadfastly on her. "None that come to mind."

"I'm glad to hear that, because I believe we've both had enough of this waiting game. You have to know how frustrating it's been denying myself these past weeks when you were doing your damnedest to charm me…then walk away. No more walking. No more waiting."

She lowered his hands back to the armrests on his oversize office chair. His eyes stroked her instead, his knuckles turning white with restraint. Good. She'd planned every moment of this on her drive over to his office, hoping she'd see the same fierce hunger in his expression that she'd been feeling for weeks.

Now, she shimmied out of her jeans, thumbing her panties down as well, the fabric teasing her skin already hungry for contact. She kicked the clothing free until she stood before him in only red spike heels and a ruby necklace.

Desire burned in his eyes, encouraging her to

continue. One slow, sultry step at a time she closed the distance between them. Bella straddled his lap, her knees on either side of his legs, and cupped his face in her hands.

Sealing her mouth to his, she kissed, nipped, tasted while brushing her breasts against his crisp white shirt. The starched fabric rubbed arousing friction against her needy nipples, the silky tie caressing sensually between her breasts, until she rocked her hips against him in desperation to ease the deeper ache. She unbuckled his belt, opened his pants and freed him to her soft and stroking touch.

His grip on the wooden armrests tightened until his biceps bulged. "Things are moving mighty fast here."

"That's only a problem if you're a one-shot kinda guy, and I happen to know from past experience with you that's not the case. So what do you say we make it fast this time to take off the edge then take things slower the next time on your desk…" She kissed the side of his mouth, breathing in his breath, locking gazes. "And on your sofa."

He pressed warm kisses down her neck that fired a trail of sweet sensation through her restless body. The chair rocked as their kisses grew more frenzied, wheeling backward until it lodged against the wall.

Drawing slightly away, she reached behind her for the condom she'd brought along, praying he had more stashed away somewhere because she actually hadn't thought further than this one time. She tore open the packet with frantic, shaking fingers until finally, after weeks of waiting, she could sheathe him with slow deliberation.

Rising up on her knees, she then eased herself onto him, taking him into her body deeper and deeper until she settled on his lap, her knees tight against his hips. Delicious shivers of pleasure prickled along her nerves.

"Enough," he growled, standing, holding her in place.

She locked her legs around his waist and looped her arms around his neck. Her desire spiked at his bold move and she dug her nails deeper into back.

Sam swept an arm over his desk in a clearing swoop to the side before lowering her onto the slick mahogany. Standing between her legs, he moved, thrust, drove them both higher with pleasure.

His hands freed and her ability to speak scattered with her thoughts, he played his fingers over her body, her breasts as she held on to furniture this time, anchoring herself in the moment, the muscle-melting sensations rising at such a rapid rate already she...

Flew apart.

Pleasure pulsed through her as she thrashed her head from side to side, biting her lip to keep from crying out. Still, he thrust, belying her words of a quick finish until he'd taken her to completion a second time. This time she couldn't control the moans of ecstasy from slipping past her lips as she arched upward and he quickly sealed his mouth to hers. He clasped her to his chest until he finished pulsing inside her, his face tight against her cheek, his growl strained between his clenched teeth.

His arms slackened and Bella collapsed back onto his desk with a gusty sigh.

"Wow, Sam, that was…Wow." She focused on the shimmering after-tingles, her heart not even close to slowing down its frantic pace.

"I agree." Bracing one hand on the desk, he smoothed her hair back from her face as he drew in ragged gasps.

She centered herself in this moment for as long as she could, drawing it out to avoid a return to rational, painful reality. Or maybe things would be all right after all. She and Sam could move into a new stage of their bizarre courtship/friendship. They could start a full-out affair that might truly lead to something more.

She turned her head to the side to kiss his wrist, then frowned. She eased up onto an elbow and reached for the discarded newspaper featuring a photo of Sam…embracing a woman she'd never seen before.

The headline blared: Garrison Cheats on Hudson, with Fiancée?

Sam buttoned his pants, pronto. Given the horror in Bella's eyes as she stared at the newspaper headline, he needed to enact damage control without delay. "I was just going to talk to you about that before we got sidetracked."

Bella scrambled off the mahogany desk and gathered her clothes at lightning speed. She yanked on her panties and jeans. "I can't believe I didn't see this coming." She whipped her strapless bra off the floor and back in place, her voice dripping with disillusionment. "I am such an idiot." She tugged her shirt over her head. "Thanks for your help this month but I'm outta here."

The burn at her quick acceptance of the worst and speedy rejection blindsided him.

"Hold on." He grabbed her wrist before she could bolt out the door. "Simmer down and let's discuss this rationally."

"Simmer down? Simmer down!" Bella jerked her arm free and stalked over to his desk. She stabbed the nearest newspaper with her finger. "What the hell is this?"

He lifted the paper and read the headline proclaiming he was cheating on Bella Hudson by seeing fiancée Tiffany Jones. The spread included a photo of him with Tiffany at a New Year's party a year ago, making it seem they'd spent *this* December thirty-first together.

The article even included a photo of a tearful, "wronged" Tiffany spilling her tale of woe, likely looking for her fifteen minutes of fame along with a hefty payoff for the article. "This is total bull. You know as well as I do how gossip rags can make things up out of thin air."

Didn't she?

Her indignation visibly ramped until her fiery hair damn near crackled with electricity. She paced restlessly, snatching her purse off the floor, her path leading her closer and closer to the door. "So you're saying this picture of the two of you super-glued together on New Year's Eve was altered?"

He scratched the kink in his neck, remembering why he hated the press so damned much. "Not exactly."

She stroked the doorknob as if already plotting her sprint away. "This picture is real?"

He hesitated.

"You *do* know her." Her hand closed around the knob. "Please don't insult me by saying she just catered the party."

He knew Bella had a temper, but he still couldn't believe she was so pissed off so fast. All her trust issues be damned, this was just an article. Irritation at her piled on top of his anger over Tiffany's stunt. Bella should know full well what the media was like. She'd grown up under the microscope herself.

He worked to keep his voice low and level. "This photo was taken a year ago when Tiffany Jones and I were seeing each other."

"Why didn't I ever hear about it?"

Her suspicious tone kicked at his already thin rein on his own temper. How had things spun out of control so damn fast? Only minutes ago they'd been locked together in a mind-numbing release.

He mentally kicked himself for not taking up this topic with her before he accepted the tempting offer she'd made when she walked in. "Not everything I do gets reported. In case you haven't noticed, I prefer to stay away from the camera's lens."

Something that had frustrated Tiffany. In hindsight, he could see she had dated him for the attention she'd thought his wealth would bring her way.

Bella released the doorknob, a sign of promising progress. "Why is she speaking out now?"

Like he was a mind reader? If that were the case he would know how the hell to reason with Bella. "For attention. For money. For revenge because I ended our engagement."

"Fiancée?" Any sign of softening disappeared in a snap, her blue eyes darting shards of ice his way. "She really was your fiancée like the paper says? When?"

"I broke it off at Thanksgiving." A very messy breakup where he'd nearly had his head taken off by a Ming Dynasty vase Tiffany had hurtled his way. Yet he hadn't even thought about her in weeks, a further affirmation he'd made the right decision in ending things with her.

"Mere weeks before you met me?" Her voice rose with each word. "We've been together for over a month now and you never thought to mention you'd been engaged?"

"We weren't planning anything serious and then I honestly didn't think of her."

She wrapped her arms around her waist defensively. "I don't believe you."

"What?" His sense of honor roared. He wouldn't deny he was ruthless, but by God, he did not cheat.

"I don't believe you." Her chin tipped, her eyes full of hurt as well as anger. "Why should I? Everyone knows your reputation with women and I chose to ignore it. Well, not anymore."

"I'm not going to stand here while you call me a liar." He turned his back, walking to his desk to put distance between them. He was not the sort of man to stare down a woman in an attempt to physically intimidate her, but he also wouldn't put up with these irrational accusations.

Sam pivoted behind his desk to face her again. "I've spent the past weeks with you in front of the press, supporting you, helping you save face while you flirted with every damn man in sight."

Her head snapped back. "What are you talking about?"

"At the parties." A month's worth of exasperation boiled to the surface. "It gets old sitting around with my thumb up my—" he cleared his throat if not his anger "—sitting around while you let other men paw you."

Her eyes went wide with shock, then she shook her head in amazement. "I could almost laugh at your jealousy, almost." Her face went emotionless and she hitched her purse higher on her shoulder as if readying to walk the hell out of his life. "It seems neither of us trusts the other and without trust we have nothing."

Bella grabbed the doorknob again, her spine regally stiff with Lillian-like poise. "Thank you for your help with the promo issues these past weeks. It's obvious our time together is over."

She opened the door and left.

Bella hitched her bag even more securely onto her shoulder and marched past Sam's secretary, head held high on her way into the hallway. She wouldn't give anyone the satisfaction of seeing her cry, especially not someone who worked for Sam and probably knew that Tiffany person.

Likely Sam had been telling the truth about breaking up with Tiffany before he and Bella met. But this made her realize just how little of himself he'd ever shared with her. All those romantic gestures through the month had simply been about getting her back in bed. She'd been such a gullible sucker. She been right to run out of his office before her still-humming body lured her back into his arms.

Construction work thundering overhead echoed the pounding in her ears. She should have known better. She'd heard about Sam's reputation as a player. She'd seen firsthand how easily relationships fell apart in her family. Yet she'd naively thought she and Sam could be different just because he'd spent four weeks wooing her.

He was simply a damn good multitasker.

Her hurt feelings over Ridley felt like nothing in comparison to the heartache jack-hammering through her now. Somehow during this past month, Sam had eased the ache of Ridley's callousness, her

parents' betrayal, and the imminent loss of her grandmother, she'd felt a certain comfort in knowing she
could lean on Sam through it all.

She'd been right to expect all or nothing, and
wrong to come over here so impulsively. Except it
hurt so damn bad to be on the nothing end of that deal.

A custodian rolled a cart down the hall, casting a
quick curious glance at her. Bella scrounged a feeble
smile and swiped away the tears she'd been so des-
perate to hold in. Her hand came back smudged with
mascara and makeup.

Damn it. She needed to get out of here.

Rushing toward the elevator, she fished in her purse
for a tissue and mirror, shuffling aside her wallet, brush,
her cell phone, a bag of doggie treats for Muffin…

Wait.

She thumbed the elevator button and backtracked
to the pink phone flashing "missed call." She stepped
into the empty elevator as she retrieved her messages.

Her brother Max's voice came over the phone.
"Bella, call me as soon as you get this message. It's
important."

Her stomach clenched. It couldn't be…. Not now.
Not yet. Not when so much of her life was falling
apart. Her fingers shook so hard she could barely
operate her cell phone as the elevator whooshed down
five floors. Finally, she connected to her brother's
number just as the door chimed on the main floor.

"Please, please, pick up," she chanted while the
phone rang.

The ringing stopped. "Bella." Max's somber voice erased all hopes of escaping the worst news. "I'm sorry, kiddo. It's Grandmother. She passed away a half hour ago."

Eleven

Three days later, Sam sat in his Marseille office, wondering why the hell he was still staring out the window at the harbor rather than getting back to work. Bella had walked out on *him*, for crying out loud. She'd even ignored the brief message he'd left on her voice mail once he'd calmed down enough to offer a neutral territory discussion.

His phone buzzed—the line used by his personal assistant. Sam jabbed the speakerphone button.

"Yes," he answered, his voice clipped and rude, he knew, but he'd asked not to be interrupted.

"There's someone on line one—a Charlotte Montcalm," Parrington announced. "She insists on speaking with you. She says it's about Ms. Bella Hudson."

Was Charlotte Hudson Montcalm calling on Bella's behalf as some kind of olive branch? He wasn't sure how he felt about third-party negotiations on something that should be between him and Bella, but he also realized he couldn't ignore the call. "Thank you, Parrington."

Sam tapped line one. "Hello, Mrs. Montcalm."

"Please, call me Charlotte."

"Charlotte, what can I do for you?"

"I'm sorry to bother you at work, but since you reached out to Alec and me about Bella last month I have to think you must care about her in some way."

"No offense meant—" he creaked back in his office chair, staring out at the harbor Bella so loved "—but this is something between Bella and me."

"I agree. But when she's hurting so much right now, more than ever after such a difficult year, I just can't keep my peace. I've learned the hard way that it doesn't help to keep my feelings to myself."

"Bella's upset?" Over their breakup?

"Our grandmother passed away three days ago. I'm unable to attend the funeral because of my pregnancy, and Bella could really use some support."

Sam creaked his chair upright. Lillian Hudson had died? How had he missed that in the news?

Perhaps because he had been avoiding newspapers—even television—like the plague since storming out of his L.A. hotel and flying back to

France. He'd been so sickened by Tiffany's drama and the heartache it caused with Bella that he damn well didn't care to see a follow-up story.

"Well," Charlotte continued, "I've said my piece. I hope you'll set aside whatever it is that's keeping you in France and be there for her right now."

Still too stunned by the news of Lillian's passing, he didn't begin to know how to respond to Charlotte's request.

"I'm very sorry for your loss," he said finally. Then ended the conversation with, "Thank you for calling."

After a cool goodbye from Charlotte, the dial tone droned over his speakerphone for…he wasn't sure how long before he stabbed the button.

Lillian Hudson had died. Even knowing this day was coming, it must be crippling to Bella. He'd viewed the special bond between the two women often enough over the past month.

Charlotte was right that Bella would need support, but she had her friend and future sister-in-law Dana. She had her brothers. She'd already made it clear she didn't want him around first in his office and then by ignoring his call….

A call that must have come right after her grandmother died.

Hell.

He shoved aside his own angry feelings long enough to think about this from Bella's perspective. She'd made it clear on the very day they'd met that she had trust issues, and with good reason. He should have realized that and pushed more assertively to be heard.

Why wasn't he fighting as hard for Bella as he would for a company? Normally, he would never back down from a little controversy. Obstacles in his path had always been new challenges to conquer. Could he have taken a page out of his mother's book, ducking out on life? His mom may have chosen a mostly solitary existence in her little beach retreat, but he'd buried himself in his work with just as effective results.

He'd cut himself off to the point he didn't hear Bella. Because if he heard her, he would have to acknowledge how damn much it would hurt to lose her. He would have to face the truth that had been nudging at the back of his brain for more than a month.

He'd fallen in love with Bella Hudson.

The last of the guests had left Hudson Manor. So many had come by to visit after Lillian's funeral, Bella had wondered if she would have to hold on to her "brave face" well into the night.

Even her best acting skills couldn't carry her through this loss much longer. Her grandmother's death had hit her even harder than she'd expected, compounded by her breakup with Sam until her heart swelled with so much hurt she wondered how much longer before it burst.

Now that the house had cleared, some of the remaining family members had decided to retire to the manor's private screening room—Charles and

Lillian's favorite feature—and watch old home movies. At least in the darkened theater she wouldn't have to hide her emotions any longer.

Thank goodness David had bowed out after the last guest left. Bella decided she really couldn't think of him as anything other than her uncle. She'd never been close to him and a simple, sad quirk of genetics wasn't going to change that. David had known he was her father all her life and chose to stay silent. She could even write that off as a man attempting to keep peace in his family, but he had also ignored her as thoroughly as he disregarded his two children with his wife.

The man truly had no feelings for his offspring. He didn't deserve anything from her. She would forgive him like her grandmother had asked, but that didn't mean she had to open her heart to a man who'd never cared for her.

First into the home studio, Bella slid down a row of luxury theater seating in the middle, pushing down her seat for the best view. She kicked off her black heels, tugged her dress over her knees and scooched down low in the deep leather chair. The whole cavernous room was decorated in black and white except for large color movie posters of the most successful Hudson Picture's films.

Her brothers filed in—Dev, Max and Luc—each hugging her on his way past. Her cousin/half brother Jack joined them, all the wives and fiancées filling seats until wow, what a legacy Lillian had left.

Suddenly everyone quieted.

Sabrina and Markus walked down the aisle, united in their grief if nothing else. They weren't touching or even looking at each other, but they were here together for their children and in honor of Lillian.

Sabrina, a strikingly handsome woman with dark blond hair and blue eyes, slid on the end beside Luc, her body stiff and defensive as if she feared being asked to leave.

Markus, distinguished but with perhaps a few extra strands of gray in his dark hair, circled round to the other side to sit beside…

Bella.

Her eyes watered and she blinked back tears before she wrecked what little makeup she had left. He patted her hand as selections from home videos of Lillian started rolling, through her early years with her husband and small children, to her years as the grandmother of a rapidly expanding family.

An image of Max in a cowboy outfit appeared, complete with chaps and a hat. Except he hadn't known to wear his jeans, and only had on little boy underwear. Much needed laughter rolled through the theater, Dana leaning closer to her fiancé, clasping his arm and smiling.

Max shook his head. "Where's the video of the summer Gran organized us all into an acting troupe? We could use some footage of Luc and Jack in tights during Gran's Shakespearean week."

More laughter echoed up to bounce around in the high ceiling. Bella couldn't help but wonder what boyhood memories Sam carried with him as an only child. He'd mentioned numerous cousins. Had they included him?

Next on the screen came a clip Bella remembered well, her seventh birthday. Grandmere had organized a Pierrot and Harlequin theme, complete with stylized clown costumes true to the era. The day stayed etched in her mind, the taste of strawberry cake, the sound of carnival music.

On the screen, a younger Markus stepped into the camera's sites, past the jugglers, carrying a scruffy little puppy with a pink Pierrot ruffle around its neck.

Seven-year-old Bella sprinted across the lawn with a high-pitched squeal, her pointy clown hat toppling to the side in her haste to hug her father and the dog—Muffin number one who had passed away just three years ago.

Without thinking, Bella clasped her father's hand as she absorbed the image of such pure love on the screen in front of her. Markus squeezed her fingers gently, turning to smile at her.

He dipped his head and said softly, "I've missed you, princess."

He'd always called her that, his princess. She hadn't realized until now how much she'd missed hearing it. Bella swallowed down the lump in her throat thicker than that long-ago cake as she thought of her grandmother's request to be kind to her father. In Bella's mind, that was Markus.

"I should have called or come straight to you," she whispered, everyone else caught up in the ongoing family video clips. "I'm sorry. I was so busy feeling sorry for myself and resenting Mom, I didn't think enough about you."

"I made my own mistakes in the marriage. It's rare that any marital trouble is only one person's fault. I just hate how this has affected you." He cleared his throat. "I miss the sparkle in my little girl's eyes."

She couldn't hold back the words and blurted quietly, "But I'm not your little girl."

"That's where you're wrong," Markus said firmly. "David may have cost me my wife, but he can never take you away. You are my daughter."

She'd felt that in her heart—known that she could never think of David as her father. But, oh God, it felt so good to hear that Markus—her daddy—felt the same way.

He opened his arms and she fell straight into his familiar embrace.

"Love you, Dad."

"Love you, too, princess." He patted her shoulders and it felt right, familiar.

Easing back into her seat, she sensed a pair of eyes watching her and her father. She searched down the row and locked gazes with her mother. Heartbreak had stamped fresh lines in her mother's face. New strands of gray streaked Sabrina's blond hair. Without question, her mother was suffering for her mistake.

Her mother wasn't perfect, but who was? They undoubtedly had a way to go in repairing their relationship after so many years of lies, but now wasn't a time for holding grudges. How strange to finally figure out at twenty-five that her parents were human, but there it was. And she loved them both.

Bella smiled across the row at her mother. A shaky smile spread across Sabrina's face in return. The tears hovering in her blue eyes glinted even from a distance in the darkened family theater.

In that moment, Bella realized it didn't matter what David had done, what her mother had done twenty-six years ago. This was her family.

A light slashed across the theater from the back, someone opening the door. Frowning, Bella looked over her shoulder and gasped.

Sam stood silhouetted in the open doorway.

Her heart swelled with something other than pain. Relief, happiness, and yes, love flooded through her as she watched him walk down the aisle, coming for her. Strong and supportive Sam who'd actually never given her any real reason to doubt him, yet she'd run at the first sign of trouble.

In a flash of inspiration she acknowledged life wasn't a matter of all or nothing, black and white issues. It was about people trying their best to love and be loved.

As she loved Sam.

* * *

Sam watched Bella rise from her seat in the dim media room. She scooted sideways past Markus toward the aisle—and she was smiling. Thank God.

He'd crossed the Atlantic, plotting his strategy the whole way for how to win her back. As he'd considered all the possible scenarios, he'd never imagined she would actually be glad to see him.

She strode barefoot toward him, her conservative black dress swishing around her knees, her high heels dangling from her fingers.

Bella stopped in front of him, her family craning to look over their shoulders. "Sam, you're here."

He kept his hands in his pockets for now. "I just heard the news about your grandmother."

"The funeral was this afternoon." She slid one shoe, then the other back on. Keeping her voice low, she spoke into his ear so as not to disturb the backdrop of children's laughter in the family video highlights splashed on the big screen.

He leaned closer to keep her openly gawking relatives from hearing. "Do you think we could go somewhere more private to talk?"

"Absolutely." She slipped her hand into the crook of his arm, turning him toward the open door.

A low buzz of whispers sounded behind them as her family huddled together. His family soon, if he had his way in winning Bella over. But even as a damn good negotiator in the business world, he knew he needed to take this one step at a time. "Where's Muffin?"

Bella glanced up. "She's in my house. I left food out and the doggie door open. I didn't think a funeral would be an appropriate place for her."

He kept his silence—as did Bella—while crossing the yard to her cottage. On impulse he stopped beside the angel fountain.

What the hell was up with that because he was never impulsive? Until now. Until Bella.

Sam turned to clasp one of her hands in his. "I truly am sorry about your grandmother."

She leaned to drag her fingers through the water, the wind blowing through the trees adding a crispness to the fifty-degree evening. "There's never a good time to say goodbye."

He shrugged out of his suit jacket and draped it over her shoulders. "I wish I could have been there for you this afternoon."

She glanced up quickly, her hand leaving the fountain to secure his jacket. "Even after how we left things?"

Was it his imagination that she'd turned her face toward his lapel and breathed deeply? Inhaling his scent?

He drank in the site of her after four days apart, cataloguing the small facets he loved about her. The restless hands that talked for her when she spoke. The red hair as vibrant as the woman herself. God, he could stand here staring at her all night, but that wouldn't get things moving.

"Do you still believe I'm hiding an engagement

to Tiffany?" No need hedging, he went straight for what mattered most. "Because there's no way I can prove when she and I broke up. You're going to have to take my word on it."

"I need you to understand I'm in a job where affairs and broken relationships are a dime a dozen. And then there's my family…"

His gut clenched as he faced the possibility she could still boot him out on his ass. "Is that a no to believing me?"

Her eyes went wide. "No. Uh, I mean no! I do believe you. I understand firsthand how bad gossip magazines can be about fabricating a whole story out of one small thread." She hugged his jacket closer. "Your actions speak louder than words. I should have believed you and I'm sorry."

"Thank you. I'm sorry too about being a jealous jackass. I may be a driven person, but I pride myself on being honest about what I want. And right from the beginning I have wanted you, Bella. It may have started out about sex, but you've got to know there's more going on between us."

He slid his hands up to cup her face, for emphasis, for her undivided attention, for the unsurpassable pleasure of simply touching her. "Bella, I've fallen in love with you."

She gasped, her eyes filling with tears.

Ah hell. He'd botched it already. "This probably wasn't the best day to spring that on you—"

She clapped a hand over his mouth. "Stop. This

is exactly what I needed to hear. Even more so, what I wanted to hear, because Sam, I was so wrong to walk out on you. I was so, so wrong to let the actions of others influence me into denying what has been growing between us these past weeks."

Bella slid her arms up and around his neck, his jacket slipping off her shoulders to the ground. "Because I have fallen in love with you, too."

Relief surged through him, driving him to lift her up for a kiss, deep, intense, echoing with a need to cement this moment and his love for her.

Bella stroked her hands over his head, down his neck, cupping his shoulders. "Sam, I do trust you, but I need to hear that you trust me, too. The whole media and schmoozing are a part of my job. Future movies will involve a love scene, so I'll be slipping into that body sock again."

He had to admit he didn't feel like cheering over that notion, but without question there would be parts of his job and life she would have to adjust to as well. They both needed to adapt. "What if I come to the studio when you're filming those scenes?"

"Hmm…" The worried pucker between her eyebrows smoothed. "I seem to recall my grandmother telling me that's what she and my grandfather did whenever she had a kissing scene in a film. I can't think of a better role model for romance than the two of them."

Her eyes filled with nostalgia and a hint of tears.

Again he regretted he hadn't been there for her earlier. But he intended to be there for her now.

And for the rest of their lives.

He thought of all she would have to get used to as well. "My main base is in Marseille and your work is based in Hollywood." He reminded himself of his vow to work as hard for her as he did for his work, harder even. "I can shift my headquarters here to the new hotel in L.A."

"Hold on." She halted him with a hand to his chest. "Does it have to be all or nothing? Could you split time between the two places? Hollywood is fun, but it would be nice to run off to France for the privacy we both crave. I even have a sister there."

"That sounds doable to me," he assured.

She would make a damn fine negotiator in the business world. They'd made a solid first step at blending their different lifestyles, giving them the time they deserved to build on the love they'd found together.

He hooked his jacket off the ground, shook it out and draped it over her shoulders again. "I stocked up on my allergy pills. What do you say we find Muffin and end this day together?"

She tucked against his side, sliding her arm around his waist. "I think that's the best proposition I've heard all year."

Epilogue

One week later

Champagne, chocolate-covered strawberries and Sam—the best way to celebrate amazing news.

Bella leaned over Sam's naked body to snag another strawberry between her teeth. She shared the plump fruit with him until they'd both nibbled their way into a sultry kiss. Given how things were still low key for the Hudsons following Lillian's funeral, Bella had opted to commemorate her exciting career milestone in a private celebration with Sam.

Sam kissed a smear of chocolate from the corner of her mouth. "Congratulations on your nomination for an Academy Award."

In addition to Bella's Best Actress nod, *Honor* had also been nominated for Best Director and Best Picture. Grandmere was no doubt cheering them on from heaven. "I'm lucky to have had such an inspiring story to enact."

Muffin yipped from her puppy bed, her new pal in a larger doggie bed beside her. Bella had surprised Sam for his birthday yesterday. She'd done some investigating about breeds of dogs that worked best for allergy sufferers. Through a pet rescue network she learned of an elderly man heading into a nursing home who couldn't keep his three-year-old Portuguese water dog. Muffin was still most definitely a fixture in their home, but now she had a more allergy friendly pal in Bear.

They had actually made quite a few changes and plans in a few short days. Bella had accepted two movie offers, a drama and comedy, both offers coming in with paychecks that put her on par with top grossing actors in Hollywood—and sent her to remote filming locales. Sam had reassured her he could use the opportunity to scout potential sites for new Garrison Grande hotels.

Plans had also been made to visit his mother's barrier island home in Southern Florida. Their lives were intertwining with seamless ease more and more each day.

Sam tugged the pink floral comforter more securely in place as he sat up. "This is supposed to be your celebration, but I sure do like my gift." He snapped his fingers. "Bear, come."

A fifty-pound mass of curly black hair, Bear re-sembled an oversized poodle. He bounded across the room, Muffin trotting at his heels. Both animals leaped onto the bed, turning circles until settling into a nest of covers.

Sam leaned back on the headboard. "Did you notice Bear's new collar?"

"It's buried in all that fur. I must have missed it."

"Check it out."

Sam really was getting into being a pet owner, something that warmed her heart. But then, Sam had a way of doing that on a regular basis.

She inched closer to the big ol' cutie and furrowed her fingers into his hypo-allergenic fur. A bright red collar peeked through, leather, but rather plain in her opinion. Still she didn't want to hurt Sam's feelings. "Very nice, and, uh, manly."

"Did you check the buckle?"

He seemed so enthused, she hung in there, twisting the collar around and found an odd lump at the buckle. "What's this?"

She looked closer. Oh, my God. A ring box.

The small black-velvet jeweler's case had blended into the color of Bear's fur. Bella's stomach tap-danced with nerves and excitement and then trepida-tion because what if this wasn't what it looked like? What if Sam had bought something else for Muffin as he'd done with the collar at the premiere of *Honor?*

It must be a new bell for Muffin's collar, she decided.

Her emotions firmly reined in, Bella untied the gift

cradled in her palm, determined to put on a happy face since Sam seemed so jazzed. They hadn't been dating long, after all, so there was plenty of time for an engagement, something she wanted more than she ever would have imagined possible a couple of months ago.

Sam slid his arm around her. "Aren't you going to open it?"

"Yes, of course." She smiled quickly and brushed a quick kiss over his lips before creaking the lid wide to reveal…

A whomping big princess-cut diamond solitaire in a gold setting.

Bella squealed and threw her arms around Sam's neck.

He laughed. "I take it that's a yes."

"Yes!" She punctuated her affirmation with a kiss, once, twice, repeating "yes" and kisses again and again. The dogs barked together, nudging her and Sam to join in the fun.

Happiness swelled inside her as Bella scooted back and held up the ring box. "Put it on my finger, please."

"My pleasure." His gray eyes twinkled as brightly as the jewel. He slid the ring slowly, reverently on her finger until it settled in place, a perfect fit. "I love you, Bella Hudson."

She smiled. "How convenient since I love you, too, Sam Garrison." She squeezed her fingers into a fist, making darn sure that ring stayed put. "I want us to do this right. Forever."

He slid an arm around her shoulder, pulling her

closer. "Obviously that's what I want, too, or I wouldn't be proposing."

She stared down at her ring, chewing her bottom lip. "Hollywood marriages have notoriously low odds."

He tipped her chin up. "I'm a whiz when it comes to the odds."

She believed him, trusted him, had faith in Sam's determination to make things happen for the best between them. Thanks to him, she also had regained her faith in forever.

Sam reached into the bedside table and pulled out two dog biscuits. He pitched one into a neat landing on Muffin's bed, followed by the second, which landed on Bear's bed.

"Well, my future wife, what do you say we finish up this celebration in style?"

Sweet anticipation curled inside her at the thought of all the celebrations ahead of them. "Again, my husband-to-be, I say yes, yes, yes." She sighed at his bold stroke up her side. *"Yes…"*

* * * * *

Can Valerie and Devlin make their marriage work?
Find out in this exclusive *short story by*
USA TODAY *bestselling author Maureen Child.*
And don't miss the last installment of the
HUDSONS OF BEVERLY HILLS,
SEDUCED INTO A PAPER MARRIAGE,
out next month on Silhouette Desire.

Scene Four

"You're leaving?" Devlin looked from the open suitcase on their bed to his wife's calm, detached expression. *"Now?"*

Val's eyes shuttered and her features were remote, deliberately blank. She only glanced at him before turning to walk to the elegant, cherrywood dresser against the far wall.

"Yes, now. There's really no point in staying any longer, is there?" Her voice was quiet, tinged with sadness, but her movements were sure, steady.

Devlin's pulse pounded until he heard the echo of his own heartbeat thundering in his ears. He hadn't expected this. Hadn't seen it coming. Though, he told himself now, he really should have.

Things hadn't been good between them from the beginning. Their marriage had gotten off to a bad start with that disastrous wedding night and had never really recovered. He spent most of his time at the studio, avoiding coming home, and Valerie was unhappy living at the family mansion. She'd wanted them to get their own place, but Devlin hadn't wanted to take the time. With all the postproduction work on *Honor*, he already had more than enough to contend with.

He hadn't loved her, but he had wanted her. Now though, sex was uncomfortable, for both of them. Since that first night, he'd never again let his own passions reign free. He'd maintained a strict control over his desires, so much so that making love to his wife was almost a formal event. A chore to be ticked off a to-do list.

She was embarrassed and uneasy, as if she knew he was holding back and so she wouldn't allow herself to fully engage in what was happening between them, either. They were two strangers who occasionally shared a bed.

Not the marriage he's envisioned, so it was hardly a shock that she wanted to leave. Though his ego was taking a beating and, damn it, she'd picked a hell of a time to acquire a backbone.

"The movie premiere is tomorrow night," he reminded her. As if she could have forgotten. It was all anyone in the family had been talking about for weeks.

"I know, and I'm sorry to miss it," she said, carefully stacking her lingerie into a corner of the suitcase. "I'm sure it'll be wonderful."

"Damn it, Val, what am I supposed to tell the family?"

She looked up at him and her eyes were filled with pain, regret and shadows of things he couldn't read or understand. "I don't care, Dev. Tell them whatever you want to tell them. This isn't about your family. This is about us. And it's just not working."

"And leaving will fix it?" He sounded unreasonable even to himself, but he didn't care.

Once the media got hold of this, he thought in disgust, the premiere of *Honor* would be lost in the sensationalism of yet another Hudson marriage disintegrating. Instantly, his mind filled with images of his parents' long-standing marriage and the indisputable fact of his mother's treachery. His own mother had cheated on Dev's father. Why in *hell* should he be surprised that his own wife was now walking out?

"I'm not trying to fix anything, Dev," Valerie said, moving now to the walk-in closet. "I don't think there's anything *to* fix."

"What's that supposed to mean?" He shoved both hands into the pockets of his slacks and glanced with irritation around the bedroom.

After his marriage, Devlin had moved Valerie into his rooms at the Hudson family mansion. The entire right wing was theirs, and with several bedrooms and sitting rooms, there was enough privacy afforded them that they might as well have been in their own home. Which, he conceded had been a bone of contention between them from the start.

But it was convenient and easy to get to work and why the hell would he want to move?

Now, he stared at the interior of his own bedroom as if it were a strange new place. Until that moment, he hadn't even noticed that Valerie—at least he assumed it had been she—had brought in Christmas decorations, hanging tiny white light around the framed paintings, red candles set in holly wreaths positioned on top of the dressers and tables and there was a cinnamony scent in the air, too. How had he not been aware of that before?

His wife stepped out of the closet with several items of clothing draped over one arm. She paused briefly, looked at him and gave him a sad smile. "Devlin, I thought you'd be happy I was leaving. You never wanted a marriage."

"Excuse me?" Fresh irritation erupted inside him. "I am the one who proposed. The one who swept you off to Vegas. The one who moved you in here— into my bed."

"Exactly," she said, shaking her head now as she walked to the bed and the open suitcase. While she packed, she told him, "We moved here. Into *your* place. Not ours. Into *your* bed. Not ours. You wanted a wife who would be some sort of decoration, I guess." She lifted one shoulder into a half-hearted shrug. "You expected me to slide into your life and not create a ripple, and I tried. Really."

"Yeah, you gave it a real try. A couple months and then you split on Christmas Eve. Do you want applause?"

Valerie sighed, closed the suitcase, zipped it shut, then pulled it off the bed to stand beside her. This was so much harder than she thought it would be. She didn't want to leave him, but staying was destroying her by inches.

Lifting her gaze to his, she took one long, last look at him. His cool-blue eyes, the shadow of dark whiskers on his cheeks, his broad shoulders and the stiff, unrelenting posture of his stance.

Her heart broke at the thought of never seeing him again. Even knowing that their marriage was a sham, that he felt nothing more for her than he would for a slightly annoying guest in his house, Valerie wanted to cry over the loss of him.

But she wouldn't.

She'd done enough crying in the last few weeks to last her a lifetime. She was finished being quiet and accommodating. She was through trying to be the wife he wanted instead of the woman she was. It was time to admit that loving him wasn't enough to build a marriage. She needed his respect. She needed him to love her back. And that was never going to happen.

"I'm sorry, Dev. Sorry to be leaving before Christmas. Before the premiere. But it's better this way and eventually you'll see that."

"Right. I'm sure. While I'm answering reporters'

questions about the breakup of my marriage instead of talking about the movie we've all sweated blood over for months, I'll remember you saying this is best."

Valerie blew out a breath and picked up her pale-pink sweater from the end of the bed. Shrugging into it, she then lifted her hair free and let it fall around her shoulders. "You're angry."

"That's a fair read of the situation."

"I understand.

"Great, thanks. Wouldn't want to be misunderstood."

His voice was sharp, sarcastic and the glitter in his eyes told her fury was crouched inside him, tightly leashed. Well, why wouldn't it be? He never allowed himself to completely relax with her. His passions—be they anger or desire—were always carefully banked. As if he couldn't be bothered to show her the *real* Devlin Hudson. As if she weren't important enough to engage him fully.

Sighing again, she said, "This is really as much my fault as yours. I never should have married you knowing you didn't love me."

He stiffened. "Love? That's what you want? Not a very trustworthy emotion to bet a life on. Look at my father. He loved my mom. She betrayed him."

That wound was still fresh and deep, Valerie saw. "There are two sides to a marriage, Devlin. Maybe you ought to talk to your father before you condemn your mom so easily."

"She broke her vows," he said, his tone stating emphatically that there was no excuse for that. "I didn't. I've been faithful to you, Valerie."

"I know that," she said. "This isn't about our sex life—this is about our *lives*. And I want more for mine."

"More than what?" He stalked around the edge of the wide bed where they'd spent so many awkward hours together. Just the memories of those encounters filled Valerie with grief for what might have been.

Every time he came to her, he was so stiff, so controlled, so damn careful, that Valerie knew he was remembering that first time. That night would *always* be between them. She hadn't been able to break through the walls Devlin had built around himself and she'd finally gotten tired of trying.

Gripping her shoulders he yanked her close, and she tipped her head back to stare into the eyes that had fascinated her right from the beginning.

"I've given you everything anyone could want, Valerie. You live in a damn mansion. You've got servants, money and the time to spend it anyway you choose. What the hell else is there?"

Valerie's heart broke a little as his demand seemed to echo around her. Keeping her gaze locked with his, she gave him a sad smile. "Oh, Devlin, don't you see? The fact that you can even ask that question is enough to prove that we have nothing."

"You're not making any sense." He let her go so suddenly, she staggered back a step or two.

"Yes I am. I only wish you could see it."

"Fine." He pushed one hand through his thick,

black hair, then waved that hand at the bedroom door. "You want to go? Then go."

Shaken, sad and holding her broken dreams close to her shattered heart, Valerie pulled up the handle on the suitcase and rolled it behind her to the door. But before she left, she turned for one last look at the man she still loved so very much.

"Devlin, I never wanted your money. Or your mansion. All I wanted was your love. Since I can't have that, there's really nothing to stay for, is there?"

Then she left and Devlin was alone.

* * * * *

*In honor of our 60th anniversary,
Harlequin® American Romance® is celebrating by
featuring an all-American male each month,
all year long with*
MEN MADE IN AMERICA!
*This June, we'll be featuring American men living
in the West.*

Here's a sneak preview of
THE CHIEF RANGER by Rebecca Winters.

*Chief Ranger Vance Rossiter has to confront the
sister of a man who died while under Vance's
watch...and also confront his attraction to her.*

"Chief Ranger Rossiter?" The sight of the woman who'd stepped inside Vance's office brought him to his feet. "I'm Rachel Darrow. Your secretary said I should come right in."

"Please," he said, walking around his desk to shake her hand. At a glance he estimated she was in her mid-twenties. Her feminine curves did wonders for the pale blue T-shirt and jeans she was wearing. "Ranger Jarvis informed me there's a young boy with you."

The unfriendly expression in her beautiful green eyes caught him off guard. "Yes," was her clipped reply. "When we arrived in Yosemite the ranger told me I couldn't go anywhere in the park until I talked to you first."

"That's right."

"Knowing you wanted this meeting to be private, he offered to show my nephew around Headquarters."

So this woman was the victim's sister.... "What's his name?"

"Nicky."

The boy who haunted Vance's dreams now had a name. "How old is he?"

"He turned six three weeks ago. Were you the man in charge when my brother and sister-in-law were killed?"

"Yes. To tell you I'm sorry for what happened couldn't begin to convey my feelings."

The woman's gaze didn't flicker. "I won't even try to describe mine. Just tell me one thing. Was their accident preventable?"

"Yes," he answered without hesitation.

"In other words, the people working under you fell asleep on your watch and two lives were snuffed out as a result."

Hearing it put like that, he had to set the record straight. "My staff had nothing to do with it. I, myself, could have prevented the loss of life."

Ms. Darrow's expression hardened. "So you admit culpability."

"Yes. I take full blame."

A look of pain crossed over her features. "You can just stand there and admit it?" Her cry echoed that of his own tortured soul.

"Yes." He sucked in his breath.

"I work for a cruise line. Aboard ship, it's the captain's responsibility to maintain rigid safety regulations. If a disaster like that had happened while he was in charge he would have been relieved of his command and never given another ship again."

Rachel Darrow couldn't know she was preaching to the converted. "If you've come to the park with the intention of bringing a lawsuit against me for negligence, maybe you should." It would only be what he deserved.

"Maybe I will."

In the next instant, she wheeled around and hurried out of his office. Vance could have gone after her, but it would cause a scene, something he was loath to do for a variety of reasons. In the first place, he needed to cool down before he approached her again.

The discovery of the Darrows' frozen bodies had affected every ranger in the park. A little boy had been orphaned—a boy whose aunt was all he had left.

* * * * *

Will Rachel allow Vance to explain—
and will she let him into her heart?
Find out in
THE CHIEF RANGER
Available June 2009 from
Harlequin® American Romance®.

We'll be spotlighting a different series every month
throughout 2009 to celebrate our 60th anniversary.

Look for Harlequin®
American Romance® in June!

Join us for a year-long celebration of the rugged
American male! From cops to cowboys—
Men Made in America has the hero
you've been dreaming about!

Look for

The Chief Ranger

by Rebecca Winters, on sale in June!

Bachelor CEO by Michele Dunaway	July
The Rodeo Rider by Roxann Delaney	August
Doctor Daddy by Jacqueline Diamond	September

Silhouette Desire

MAN of the MONTH

USA TODAY bestselling author

ANN MAJOR

THE BRIDE HUNTER

Former marine turned P.I. Connor Storm
is hired to find the long-lost Golden Spurs
heiress, Rebecca Collins, aka Anna Barton.
Once Connor finds her, desire takes over and
he marries her within two weeks! On their
wedding night he reveals he knows her true
identity and she flees. When he finds her
again, can he convince her that the love they
share is worth fighting for?

**Available June
wherever books are sold.**

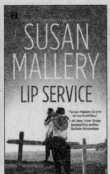
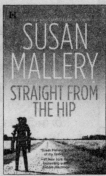

You're invited to join our Tell Harlequin Reader Panel!

By joining our new reader panel you will:

- Receive Harlequin® books—they are FREE and yours to keep with no obligation to purchase anything!
- Participate in fun online surveys
- Exchange opinions and ideas with women just like you
- Have a say in our new book ideas and help us publish the best in women's fiction

In addition, you will have a chance to win great prizes and receive special gifts! See Web site for details. Some conditions apply. Space is limited.

To join, visit us at

www.TellHarlequin.com.

REQUEST YOUR FREE BOOKS!

2 FREE NOVELS PLUS 2 FREE GIFTS!

Silhouette® *Desire*®

Passionate, Powerful, Provocative!

YES! Please send me 2 FREE Silhouette Desire® novels and my 2 FREE gifts (gifts are worth about $10). After receiving them, if I don't wish to receive any more books, I can return the shipping statement marked "cancel". If I don't cancel, I will receive 6 brand-new novels every month and be billed just $4.05 per book in the U.S. or $4.74 per book in Canada. That's a savings of almost 15% off the cover price! It's quite a bargain! Shipping and handling is just 50¢ per book.* I understand that accepting the 2 free books and gifts places me under no obligation to buy anything. I can always return a shipment and cancel at any time. Even if I never buy another book, the two free books and gifts are mine to keep forever.   225 SDN EYMS 326 SDN EYM4

Name _____ (PLEASE PRINT)

Address _____ Apt. # _____

City _____ State/Prov. _____ Zip/Postal Code _____

Signature (if under 18, a parent or guardian must sign)

Mail to the **Silhouette Reader Service:**
IN U.S.A.: P.O. Box 1867, Buffalo, NY 14240-1867
IN CANADA: P.O. Box 609, Fort Erie, Ontario L2A 5X3

Not valid to current subscribers of Silhouette Desire books.

Want to try two free books from another line?
Call 1-800-873-8635 or visit www.morefreebooks.com.

* Terms and prices subject to change without notice. Prices do not include applicable taxes. Sales tax applicable in N.Y. Canadian residents will be charged applicable provincial taxes and GST. Offer not valid in Quebec. This offer is limited to one order per household. All orders subject to approval. Credit or debit balances in a customer's account(s) may be offset by any other outstanding balance owed by or to the customer. Please allow 4 to 6 weeks for delivery. Offer available while quantities last.

Your Privacy: Silhouette Books is committed to protecting your privacy. Our Privacy Policy is available online at www.eHarlequin.com or upon request from the Reader Service. From time to time we make our lists of customers available to reputable third parties who may have a product or service of interest to you. If you would prefer we not share your name and address, please check here. ☐

SDES09R